Arky Types

Other books by

Sara Maitland

Introduction 5
Daughter of Jerusalem
Map of the New Country: Women and Christianity
Telling Tales
Virgin Territory
Vesta Tilley
A Book of Spells
Walking on the Water (editor)
Tales I Tell My Mother (co-author)
More Tales I Tell My Mother (co-author)
Weddings and Funerals (co-author)

Michelene Wandor

Gardens of Eden
Five Plays
Guests in the Body
Carry On, Understudies
Look Back in Gender*
Plays by Women, Vols 1–4 (editor)*
On Gender and Writing (editor and contributor)
Tales I Tell My Mother (co-author)
More Tales I Tell My Mother (co-author)

*available from Methuen

Sara Maitland and Michelene Wandor

ARKY TYPES

Methuen

First published in Great Britain 1987
by Methuen London Ltd
11 New Fetter Lane, London EC4P 4EE

Printed and bound in Great Britain by
Richard Clay Ltd, Bungay, Suffolk

British Library Cataloguing in Publication Data

Maitland, Sara
Arky types.
I. Title II. Wandor, Michelene
823'.914[F] PR6063.A355

ISBN 0-413-16400-4

Arky Types

Dear Michelene Wandor and Sarah Maitland,

I was at the York Literary Festival last week and heard the two of you do your extraordinary (in the best possible sense of the word) reading.

Of course I have known both of you by reputation for some years, but have never felt brave enough to approach you directly. There are a lot of publishers wanting to ride the women's bandwagon and I am not too proud to admit that I am one of them, but I have seldom been moved to commission on spec like this before. I think you have both reached a career point where the use of the word feminist is ceasing to be flattering and becoming limiting. So I'm emboldened now to make a suggestion. I was interested in how you both spoke with such conviction about the ways in which writers could and did use each other's imaginations. Would you be interested in taking this one stage further and writing a fiction together?

To allay your probable doubts I should say that I am not among those editors who want to dictate to their writers: you would feel that you had a completely free rein, though obviously I should be fascinated, and probably educated, to hear whatever ideas you might cook up.

I am sure that I don't have to tell you how the market for intelligent women's fiction has opened up, and of course I accept and appreciate your political commitments to feminism, but I don't think you should feel bound by any literary or political orthodoxies.

If you want to talk about this further, that is one of the things I am here for; let me know if the idea appeals to you as much as it does to all of us here. I know you can write a fascinating book.

With admiration, yours sincerely,
N Mason, Editorial Director

Dear Nicky,

Sara (note the spelling) and Michelene tell me that you have approached them about commissioning a work of joint fiction from them. May I congratulate you on your initiative and insight. They have such a good (if specialized) track record between them that I know they will come up with something unusual and, I am sure, very commercial.

On the assumption that the project has already ground its way through your editorial machinery, let's talk about an offer that takes proper cognisance of the fact that this will undoubtedly be a very commercial enterprise – I'll be in Suffolk over the weekend, but back in the office on Monday.

Yours etc . . .
Sam Smith

Dear Sara and Michelene,

I am waiting for an offer from Nicky. I should warn you that I don't expect that it will be very much; it is, let's face it, the sort of book that has an audience of one, as we say in the trade. But I will, of course, do my best.

Best, Sam

Dear Ms Maitland,

I hope you don't mind me writing to you. A friend sent me a copy of a book of short stories,* and one of them seems to be about my great-great-great-great-great- (I think that's right) grandmother – the 'dwarf'. Please forgive me if this is impertinent, but I would like to know how you got hold of her diaries. After she died, the diaries were lost until about the middle of the nineteenth century, when they came back into the family. As far as we know, no one else has ever seen the diaries. After her child was born – a daughter, and alive, although only just, after the horrific childbirth, forceps, etc – she went into service in London, and also toured for a while in a sort of circus – really a kind of freak-show thing, as you can imagine. Her daughter was 'normal' – well, whatever we mean by the word – and although she was only about four feet tall, she was not in any other way disabled.

I must be honest; I could not bear to read your story. I have read those words so many times in the diaries, and have always felt it to be my own private horror, my own memory of what she suffered and could not tell, and I feel very funny seeing it all in print like that, for anyone to read. Perhaps you just came across the diaries somewhere, and didn't realize what they were. That is probably it, because you don't mention her name, you just call her the 'dwarf'. She was called Françoise, and I am sort of named after her – my name is Frances, but everyone calls me Frankie. Although it all happened a long time ago, and although none of the family is now what you would call a dwarf, I have always felt I was on

* *Weddings and Funerals*, Sara Maitland and Aileen La Tourette (Brilliance Books, 1984)

show, but this is my choice, as I am a dancer and I love it.

I will stop now because I have to go to rehearsal.

Where did you get the diaries? Could you please reply c/o Michelene, who is a sort of acquaintance, because I am going off on tour and won't have a settled address for a while.

Yours, Frankie Summers

My dear Michelene,

I've had a slightly odd letter from a friend of yours, or rather 'a sort of acquaintance'. I can't help wondering if she's OK. She's written very interestingly about the Forceps Delivery story. What makes me wonder a bit about her is that her story really doesn't correspond to the known facts. Mariceau, the doctor on the case, wrote the case up quite fully and includes the information that he performed a postmortem Caesarian on his patient and discovered a dead 'male child' still *in utero* although he acknowledged with some admiration that Chamberlen had managed to engage the head. Now (although I'm not deeply addicted to conspiracy theory) it is possible that he and Chamberlen cooked up this story, because if there had been any chance of the child being born alive then they acted with extraordinary irresponsibility towards their patient; but most of the obstetric evidence of the times does not suggest that the doctors really took the issue of medical responsibility very seriously. Frankie says that she's a descendant of the woman in the story. If this is true then I should, of course, be fascinated to hear more about it.

Anyway, I've written her a letter, and since you know her I'd be grateful if you could forward it to her.

Love as always, Sara

Dear Sara,

Thanks for your note. I've forwarded your letter to Frankie, who is at the moment somewhere in the Black Country, on tour.

I met her in Newcastle last year when I did a rather grotty poetry reading in a community centre there. It wasn't anyone's fault that the reading was grotty – it was one of those places that has a regular and secure little coterie of writers who meet and talk and drink and write and read and have all their rivalries and what-have-you, and even though they regularly invite outside readers down, you feel as if you're intruding into some kind of family when you get there. So you feel either you've got to be a star and just revered as 'great', or you have to prove yourself to be better, or at least more interesting, than any of them to justify your intrusion and the money they're paying you. After the reading, there was a desultory sort of discussion, and a middle-aged man took issue with me about feminism and produced the usual blah about how you couldn't produce art and be political. When he left I noticed that he was with a much younger woman with long dark hair, swept back, no fringe, a black beret and bright red lipstick. She was quite striking and I remember wondering whether he was her father, or whether she was an old-style groupie – or what?

Anyway, she wrote to me (don't know where she got my address) and sent me some poems. Being a conscientious sort of soul, I wrote back, just making the usual sort of encouraging noises, and then she turned up on my doorstep one afternoon, saying she wanted to talk to me. You know how bloody possessive I am about my territory (ie, home), but I invited her in (I really am bored to tears with all this factual stuff) and she stayed the night. On the couch. She talked about poetry, she talked a bit about her work.

She sent me a bunch of flowers in thanks, and then she's been sending me postcards from various places since.

I don't think she's bad or anything, but she has a way of making do in the world which involves telling different stories at different times. I am not at all like that myself, and so I am both very jealous and suspicious of someone who is. Maybe I'm just jealous that she wrote to you and is using me as a go-between. However, I'm also intrigued, so I don't mind taking on that role for the time being. As to your question about whether she's OK – well, I think she's looking for something but I'm not sure what. After that, your guess is as good as mine. Or maybe better.

See you next week, Michelene

Dear Frankie Summers,

Thank you so much for your interesting letter. Of course it's not impertinent, but it is very difficult to answer. Difficult because I don't actually think I have *seen* your foremother's diaries, although I am an obsessive reader of oddly encountered things: Shakespeare's 'picker up of unconsidered trifles'. And also a dangerous magpie. So . . . I don't like the charge of plagiarism or theft and I'm never completely sure that it isn't justified.

Perhaps if I told you how I came by the text it might be helpful to us both. I first made Françoise's acquaintance in a book by Adrienne Rich called *Of Woman Born*;* talking about the history of medical intervention in childbirth she goes in some detail into the highly dubious activities of the Chamberlen family which includes obviously a very brief account of your foremother's 'case'.

It was interesting; but then she (Rich) did the most dreadful thing: in a footnote she pointed out (rightly) that Françoise (I think I'll have to take the liberty of calling her that, please) was a nameless victim of medical experimentation, but then said that as dwarf she must have been a rape victim. I thought that was outrageous and a final writing off of the autonomy of freaks (the reason why I even use this word will I think emerge) who are apparently not even allowed a sexual life of their own. As a story, a horror story, the whole thing hung around in my head and I did some further background reading; there isn't a lot but there is some, though all of it from the point of view of the 'progress' of science, nothing about her as a person, or her as dwarf

* *Of Woman Born*, Adrienne Rich (Virago, 1977)

either. Anyway here was a story, sitting around unformed but *there*.

Then, several years ago and for a variety of reasons – most of them distressing and none of them very interesting at this point – I became aware of how much all feminist women, which includes me, seem at some psychic level to be convinced of their own freakishness, that feminism itself – although at another level politically rational and sensible and sound – is a consolation for, a desperate effort to obliterate our own self-conviction of being freaks. We are freaks; and dwarves – because of their role in folk literature in Northern Europe – are a particularly good literary image of our own freakishness. We are freaks, we are dwarves, and we fear that in ourselves (the 'better-out-than-in-let's-talk-about-it' discourse that pervades feminism obviously ties up with the image of the dwarf in labour although I hadn't made that connection until now). Everyone is a freak. And the freak in all of us is a painful thing to carry around. It was my dwarf not your dwarf whose voice I was trying to catch in the story.

What is difficult here is that, given that the externals of my story come from other places, how can I be sure that I *haven't* seen your dwarf's diaries, and haven't simply stolen them from you? I do understand your protectiveness of her, and through her of yourself, and particularly the feeling that stuff is being stolen from you, from your history and perhaps from your need. I too feel defensive about *my* story, *my* dwarf and *my* right to use that – this really is an important concern to do with community and trust and with how people steal one's ideas.

Given these correspondences, of course I am interested in the story of your life. I would be deeply grateful if you felt that I could see some of the diary in a more open way. Have you discussed any of this with Michelene? I know she is interested in the same sorts of issues and is particularly sensitive about the social ownership of individual material. I'm not clear how well you know her, but perhaps when you get back from your tour the three of us could get together and try and talk through some of it.

I would like to add that it is rather unusual for me to write to total strangers like this. Perhaps your friendship with someone whom I think of as a special person and very special friend has something to do with it; but so also does your own letter, which is touching at rather a lot of levels (I mean it touches *me*).

I shall hope to hear from you again when you're ready.

Yours, Sara Maitland

Dear Nicky,

I really think you need not worry. Sara and Michelene are not interested in simply producing another ghetto book. Whether they or you will want to use the term 'feminist' is of course something you will sort out between you, when there is a manuscript to discuss. Meanwhile, may I reiterate that their intention is to write something of wide, nay even popular, appeal, and given your projected print run during our conversation on Monday, I thought you had accepted that as realistic.

I think you should up your offer by at least 50%. I would, as is customary in our negotiations, retain American rights.

I must say I am looking forward to selling you a book. It's been a long time.

Best wishes, Sam

Dear Sam,

Thank you for your note. I think you are exaggerating my worries a bit: of course I'm sure that your two don't want to write a ghetto book. As you say in your letter, our projected print run proves our commitment to the project. I know it will be an extremely exciting book.

Which said, I do think you have to be a bit realistic. It is expecting a bit much if you want me to go to my overlords in the accounts department and ask them to pay the sort of money you are talking about to two authors they will never have heard of, who can't give us a proper option clause on their next real books, for a book that has no subject matter, no content – indeed, as far as we know so far, no anything I can show them. And then to tell them that they can't even have the US rights! I've always appreciated the way you do go all out for your authors, but it might be in Sara's and Michelene's own real interests to make clear to them that I'm not a free agent in all this, and I cannot wring money from a stone for a book as nebulous as this.

If you're adamant about a bit more cash on the table, perhaps you could persuade them to do me an outline or something.

In the meantime, I've heard on the grapevine that you've got your hands on the memoirs of the gorgeous Fraülein B – true?? – honestly, I don't know how you do it. If so, remember your old comrade and friend; you're right, it is high time you sold me a book.

Obviously with Frankfurt coming up I'm up to my eyes; but I do want Michelene and Sara's book, rather a lot; I do think they are both worth some investment at this stage, and I am formally interested in the idea of a joint fiction – not only fun but something I believe in the possibility of . . . BUT business is business, and I cannot justify the sort of money that you seem to be thinking about.

Best wishes, Nicky

Dear Sara and Michelene,

Nicky's heels seem to be dug in, I'm afraid. I can't squeeze another shekel, though there was a mutter about your producing a sample chapter. I muttered back that it was not our initiative in the first place, and it wasn't reasonable to expect you to produce a sample chapter. It looks like stalemate, but I'll have one more try.

Best, Sam

Dear Ms Wandor,

I am writing to ask you a favour. I am an academic theologian, with a specialism in Biblical Studies. Normally I teach here at St Alphege Seminary, which is a Roman Catholic Institution affiliated to London University. However, given the growth of interest in Feminist Theology, we have decided to give a special course of open lectures in conjunction with a small group of more feminist women, including Christian feminists, and some feminist historians. The theme of the lectures is 'The Representation of Women in Christianity' and I have been delegated to invite the speakers. The organizing committee are all very enthusiastic that I should invite you to give one of the eight talks in this series.

Earlier in the year I heard some of your poems from your book, *Gardens of Eden*.* They were part of a paper given by a slightly eccentric maverick theologian called Sara Maitland, who was addressing the ways in which contemporary theological language might name or image God. I was deeply struck by the poem about abstract art. Subsequently, I bought the book and was even more struck. I admit I'm not a great poetry reader so the jokes did help, but I was intrigued, very seriously, by some of the more profound questions you raise, from a theological/philosophical angle: particularly about the relationship of text and context, and also how we can address the biblical imagery, ethics, etc, given the completely changed social data. Because of course, while we all say in one mode or another that 'abstract art must truly be divine', that 'God is without qualities', we all – as you do – go on naming Him

* *Gardens of Eden*, Michelene Wandor (Journeyman, 1984)

(sorry, I'm trying with that one; I do appreciate the feminist line) God in very real material unabstract formulations.

This is offered as some explanation of why I'm writing to you. The course details are still flexible. I want the lectures to make a break with traditional theological styles; if you just wanted to read and perhaps explain a little how and why you came to write these poems it would be wonderful. Incidentally, I'm assuming from the poems that you are Jewish; I would actually consider this an advantage in a course of this kind.

Yours sincerely,
Sr Mary Clare, OSW, Dean of Biblical Studies.

Dear Sr Mary Clare,

Forgive me if I have addressed you incorrectly; I don't believe I have ever spoken to a nun before, much less written a letter to one, and I just am simply not sure of the right way to address you. Are you like royalty, so that I have to use your title all the time, or do I just call you 'Sr' (what does that stand for anyway?) until I know you well enough to call you Mary – anyway, this chatter is really a grateful response to the fact that you like my poems in *Gardens of Eden*.

I would be very pleased indeed to come and contribute something to your course on 'Women in Christianity'. Ideally, I'd like to be able to read the poems, interspersed with some chat and explanation, followed by discussion if you think that would be useful. I have done that as a format in the past (indeed, am doing it this coming weekend) and it goes down very well. So let me know about that.

I must confess that your invitation gave me great pleasure and also induced some nervousness. You see, I don't know how my scepticism might go down with your audience. Secondly, I am Jewish, (your assumption was correct) and have very recently discovered that, however mixed my responses are, I am feeling a little proprietorial towards the Old Testament. I suppose that is not really surprising, since Judaism begins and ends with the Old, whereas Christianity begins with the New but appropriates the Old in whatever ways it wishes. But given all this, I would be absolutely fascinated to see what a religious/theological audience would make of my readings, and be most intrigued to hear what questions you think are raised by the poems from a theological/philosophical angel. A good mistype, that. I meant, of course, Angle. Which approaches the word Anglican –

are you, like Sara, an Anglican? Is that a silly question?

By the way, are you able to pay any kind of fee? You didn't mention it in your letter.

If the above hasn't changed your mind, do let me know what possible dates you have in mind. My time is fairly flexible, but one or two evenings in the week are already regularly promised.

Thanks for writing and I look forward to hearing from you.

Yours, Michelene Wandor

Dear Michelene Wandor,

Thank you for your open letter. In theory the lectures are scheduled for Wednesday evenings from the 24th October for eight weeks, with more after Xmas. Wednesday the 7th, 14th or 21st November would all be suitable from my point of view for you to come. Can you let me know if you have any marked preferences. The lectures would begin at 7.30. Essentially the class would consist of theological students – the usual slightly mixed bag, trainee priests, some women religious, plus the wider 'market' of concerned feminists. We may, depending on the quality of the speakers I can get, advertise them more widely; but we'd expect about forty to fifty people to be there. One of the lectures, on women and the prophetic tradition with reference to the Sophia literature, I shall be giving myself; all the others will be invited from outside so you won't be alone.

I'm sorry we did not mention the matter of a fee. A churchy slip there, we all get too used to pretending that everyone does everything for love: this is really because we're so clericized, and of course all clergy draw their pay whatever they decide to do with their time. Of course we can offer you a fee, although perhaps not as large as you might hope. £45 is our standard for this sort of lecture, but I might be able to find some more if this is not enough for you. Can you let me know?

Perhaps this is not the time to take it up but I was very interested in what you said about Christianity 'appropriating' the Old Testament, because of course this is not the way we see it. We do not see Christianity as 'beginning with the new' you see, but as a continuum of revelation, so that Christ was born 'in the fullness of time'. For a lot of Christians this is a tricky area because we cannot any more be unaware of the ways in which the church 'invented' anti-semitism and of the weight of responsibility for that. And anti-semitism remains, of course, so that it is now difficult to articulate the orthodox relationship to the whole canon of scripture, particularly given the Church's traditional claim to have the authority to interpret the whole meaning of the text (in one sense the Church has always been 'modernist' in that it has always known that the text needed interpretation, as opposed to fundamentalists who think that it can be read without cultural prejudice afresh each time'. On the other hand, our claims of authority (eg, our claim that the promises of the prophets are fulfilled in the life of Jesus) are inevitably expressed in terms which must indeed be very offensive. Trying to read the texts within their own *sitz in Leben* is difficult indeed. The conflicting roots of early Christianity within Judaism and within Hellenism, and the contradictions that raises, are well described by other theologians: but that does not solve the problem. This certainly is one of the areas of theological/philosophical enquiry which *Gardens of Eden* raises: the Jewish Momma figure (if I may use the expression at all) is after all a product of the social circumstances of being Jewish in the dominant Christian *and anti-semitic* culture, so how can we imagine at all the experience of being Jewish in the odd historical circumstances of an enclosed, threatened but triumphing culture say of the time of the Kingdom? And for Christians it is important to try because it was that understanding of God which formed our own, and in particular formed Jesus's. Jesus was a Jew, and a pre-Christian Jew at that. Do you see?

Anyway, you probably have far more important things to do than listen to this sort of questioning by a middle-aged nun. I'm sure that it is not your problem to help me with my residual anti-semitism, especially within theoretical constructs of theology, since you say you are an atheist (are you sure by the way? can an artist be an atheist?). To return to the point: your outline for your talk sounds excellent and exactly what I had hoped for. If you want any specific briefing on the expectations of a religious/theological audience do please ask. And let me know if the fee and the date are suitable.

With many thanks, Sr Mary Clare, OSW

PS Sr stands for Sister just as Mr stands for Mister. Your address was therefore absolutely correct. In speech it is usual to say Sister, or Sister Mary Clare. We don't have surnames. OSW stands for Order of St Walburga. If Sister sticks in your throat you could call me Clare (not Mary – all the Sisters in my Order have Mary before their name) but I might well not answer because no one does. My 'natural family' calls me Anita still – my name before I entered – and everyone else calls me Sister, I think. Does that seem very strange to you? And, no, I'm not an Anglican but a Roman Catholic; there are not very many Anglican religious (the technical name for nuns). If you want to know more about it, really the best thing I can recommend is the chapter on women religious in Sara Maitland's book *A Map of the New Country*,* which is, though over optimistic and generous, rather good. Which brings me to what I hope will be the last point: I did not realize when I wrote to you that you *knew* Sara Maitland. I hope I said nothing unkind.

* *A Map of the New Country*, Sara Maitland (Routledge, 1983)

Dear Sam,

Michelene is away so I can't get in touch with her, BUT I am reasonably certain that she would agree with me that this whole thing is ridiculous. We aren't going to write an outline or sample chapter because we're not working that way. And because Nicky initiated the whole project. I don't understand what is going on; if they wanted the book – and we showed you the invitatory letter – they must have thought about paying for it then (??). Next Nicky will be wanting to dictate the whole damn thing. Why not indeed? But leave us out of it. You are better placed than I am to know how far you can push this, but if this is typical of the carry-on we're going to get, I can't help wondering if it's all going to be worth it whatever the money.

Anyway we'll be in touch when M gets back, this is just an instant response. Please don't commit us to an outline. OK?

I'll talk to you soon.

Love, Sara

Dear Sara,

Got your message on my answering machine when I got back. I am totally with you on this business of sample bloody chapters. Either they think we're writers or they don't. Also, in my experience, when people ask you for trial chapters, or scenes, they always cover themselves by saying 'of course, we know it may not bear any resemblance to the final thing, but . . .' in which case the only answer to it is 'in that case, let's not bother.'

One thing, though – do you think it might be better if in general we reply to Nicky together? I know it may be hard, since you're dealing with Sam over other things and I'm not, but it would at least mean they couldn't quote one of us to the other if they wanted to divide and rule. Paranoia, eh? But I never believe a commission until it's signed and the first part of the advance paid. And never write a line until it is.

Although having said that, it can do no harm for us to be DISCUSSING the book. Have you had any thoughts?

Love, Michelene

Mrs Vicar,

Fuck it.

First my Dresden ornaments got broken, smashed to smithereens, some sodding bastard shit swept them off the mantelpiece, and now the goddam tortoises have gone missing and I've only just brought them out from hibernation, and they were perfectly alright all winter, and they NEVER leave the garden, and I'm up to my damn eyes putting food in the deep freeze and getting the passports sorted out and making up the orders for the food, and you can't believe how fussy the anteaters are when they travel, and all three boys are lying around the house smoking cactus leaves all day and doing fuck-all, the giraffe is about to have a baby which means building an extra bit on to it all, Noah's off his food and isn't drinking enough water for his body weight, and the fucking gerbils have decided to sulk.

Have you seen my tortoises?

This letter was meant just to be a polite apology for not coming to your parish party for Corpus Christi. I would have, honest, even though it's not my scene, but the children get on so well, don't they. I just wondered whether you could hang on to the tortoises if they come into your garden.

Your neighbour, Mrs Noah

PS The immersion heater is leaking; do you know a good plumber?

Dear Sara,

Hot foot, damn it, I am having ideas . . . what about having one of the characters as Mrs Noah? I know virtually nothing about her, but everywhere I look there seem to be books about the Ark and all who sail in her. Why not rehabilitate the lady wife herself. The thought just popped into my head . . .

Love, Michelene

My dear Michelene,

Hang on a moment. You're two letters up on me and about six hundred miles in front of me.

Yes, I entirely agree that we should only communicate with Nicky jointly. With Sam it is a bit more difficult because we are working together on a couple of other things as you know and because we are, as it happens, old friends. Obviously, therefore I think your paranoia is misplaced! I know I'm a terrific blabbermouth and tend to chatter away about a good deal too much, but I will try, and I will certainly promise to make no commitments on 'our' behalf. I just wish to God they'd get the whole thing sorted out – apart from anything else I could use the cash and I also don't think it's good for or fair on us at this stage of a complicated project to be messed about like this. Frankly I trust Nicky about as far as a myopic mole can see, but I do want to do the book with you A LOT.

At the same time I find it bloody hard to think about it when the whole thing is left up in the air like this, and I don't want to be rushed, even by you – so if what follows is very negative I'm sorry but I'm feeling deflated by the whole thing – by next time we talk I'll probably be bouncing round all uppity and excited . . . in the meantime – why Mrs Noah for heaven's sake? Yes, I've noticed too that the story of the Ark seems to be a recurrent image for the frailty of our times, and in fact someone was saying to me the other day that this was almost inevitable at this sorry moment; and of course myth images are my bread and butter, BUT – but I suppose I feel you're dictating to my imagination, and my imagination is digging in her heels. I don't want to do satire really and I don't see how we could take such a character and not satirize her, that's the first thing. The second thing is probably more important and it is about our cultural differences, or rather about my religious feelings, and about letting you own that material – I mean it was alright (very all right) in *Gardens of Eden* because that was your own and I loved it as you know, but if you want to do knockabout comedy or religious debunking under my name then I do have difficulties with that and it needs more talking through. Thirdly I think there is a wild structural problem: if you are proposing that one of us should take Mrs Noah as a character then that will, I suppose, have to be balanced by another character and who could that be? I bet if I offered you the Virgin Mary or St Anne or even Mary Magdalene (an interesting way of addressing both the problems outlined above to take a New Testament character and an Old Testament one) you'd have a fit and if you didn't I probably would. Looking for a character of similar weight from a different tradition I find myself foxed – you can't counterweight the Old Testament stories with those from any other tradition that I know of. Snow White, or her stepmother, or Persephone, or Helen of Troy – they're all heavyweight typologies but they aren't the same, or at least I could not bring to them the weight of affectionate humour and ideological ownership that I could to a biblical character. I absolutely do not want to take two Old Testament personalities because you did that in *Gardens of Eden* and it doesn't seem fair in either direction to do it again.

Also what sort of fiction are we wanting to do? I know that it will have to be something showy (not used negatively); but beyond that, do you have any idea how we can structure something so that we can both maintain individual voices while not maintaining individual control over the plot?

Can't you hang on a little until I've caught up with you? I'll find this easier once the contract is sorted out but if you're feeling frisky I'll try and get going, in my head at least.

Sorry to be such a drag.

Love, Sara

Dear Nicky,

I gather that Michelene is proving a little sticky about the sample chapter. I'll see if I can get Sara to persuade her.

Of course I understand your in-house difficulties. But I am sure we can find a way round it if things prove difficult at the writing end. And you did initiate the project. Surely that will carry some weight (the weight of your passionate belief in the book/project) with those upstairs.

I assume we shall meet in the bustle of Frankfurt. Do you have a moment for a quiet drink, if not dinner? We can put this on the agenda then.

See you across the water.

Best wishes, Sam

Dear Sara,

Thank you for answering me. I have been feeling guilty about invading your privacy. I haven't read Adrienne Rich. Perhaps she saw the diaries somewhere. Perhaps I could write and ask her. I think you are right about Françoise about one thing, because I have a letter from her about her lover – I mean, I have a letter which she wrote to her lover, and seems not to have sent, but there are other letters as well, from him, which show that their love was very important to both of them, but it was all kept very secret. Of course I don't really know whether the awful experience you describe actually did produce a live baby, which survived, or whether it was an earlier or subsequent child.

But anyway, maybe I will show you the letters – they're in English, although a bit difficult to read.

I feel I want to protect Françoise and her history, because I think her experience is richer than any story anyone can make of it. But then at other times I feel that a story is only known when it is written down and that must make it richer, because then it can be read by other people. That is why the story has to be right, and the same as well as different.

Maybe also I found your story was richer than the diaries, because it frightened me so much. It frightened me more than the diaries because it was the same and different. I had read it before but I had not read it before.

This is probably a silly letter. I sprained my ankle in the last show of the tour, so it's giving me time to think silly things. I'm going to Brighton to stay with a friend till it gets better. Then I've got another job in summer rep. I won't tell you what it is because you'll probably disapprove. Michelene would if she knew. She's a bit the sort of person whose approval you want, but then she also makes you feel defiant. Well, she's a bit funny. I hope you don't mind me saying that because she's your friend.

Best wishes, Frankie Summers

Dear Frankie,

Thank you for your recent letter; I'm sorry about your ankle and I hope it's getting better now. Brighton is a good place to go and get better. The Pavilion is one of my favourite architectural things in all England – it has enough self-irony to get away with itself.

Actually, I am happy to get your letter and answer your questions because they are my questions too, and sometimes it helps to work things out if you try and explain them to someone else. In relation to which there is something I want to say, though it shouldn't stop you writing to Adrienne Rich if you want to – she's an American poet and a very fine one. Honestly I don't think that anyone has seen your diaries – or rather, Françoise's diaries. I don't think you will resolve your problem like that, running round looking for a 'leak'. I don't think you can claim her as your own, keep her to yourself like that. She existed in history and her life is disseminated to lots and lots of us through lots and lots of channels. Her diaries are just one of those.

But this is just me riding my hobby-horse. The other evening I had supper with some other writers and said that it always made me happy when I found that other people were writing about the same things as me because that meant that I was writing about the things that mattered to other people too. Two of the other writers thought this was very odd indeed, that when they were writing fiction they were scared all the time that other people might write their stories; perhaps I'm just arrogant, but I really don't think you can take stories away from other people, only add to them. That is why I don't often 'make up' stories of my own. I do in novels because I don't yet quite have the courage or impertinence not to, but I seldom do in short stories because I actually want to get that response which you gave me – thank you: 'It was the same and different. I had read it before but I had not read it before.' But all this does make the problem that you raised in your first letter – did I make it up? did I steal it? – rather real. So in the end I don't know.

Sometimes I think that Jung is right and we all carry the voices of all the stories round in our very blood cells, born into us at conception, along with other genetic characteristics, and other times I know that this is completely wrong and the stories are cultural and only shared to a very limited extent. When I went to Zimbabwe a couple of years ago I realized that none of my stories were yet the stories of women there, though I would really like them to be one day – I don't mean they should learn my stories but that I should find the story that was their story as well as my story and our story. It was a difficult visit all round in that sense. I lost confidence in the power of the stories to get through it all. But other times I feel hopeful, not that the stories will come to me as though by magic but that I can dig down and find them, not pre-existent in any sense, but embryonic. Traditionally dwarves are miners you know, they dig for gold in the dark belly of the earth; this is the positive side of the dwarf, but I haven't yet located that story or at any rate the way to tell it.

Oh dear, I am going on rather. I'm sorry. Perhaps stuck in Brighton this will at least give you something to laugh at – the mad feminist who sends you interminable letters. Let me know if you are likely to be in London and we could perhaps get together for a drink. Of course, I very very much want to see the diaries.

Best wishes, Sara

My dear Mrs Noah,

Thank you for your kind letter. Do not worry about the Corpus Christi party – these 'do's' are usually for our own people anyway, though of course you – and your children – are always welcome.

I am concerned by the tone of your letter; I have tried to visit several times, but you are never in; also it is a little difficult to approach your house. DIY is a good hobby for a man but you mustn't let his enthusiasm run away with him altogether. Be that as it may, I have asked the local social services to call, please don't think I'm interfering, of course, but your letter read – to me – like a cry for help. The social workers are all very nice.

As for the plumber, the Disabled Amateurs Inc (of which I am the Hon. President) do excellent work. I have asked them to call too. I am also praying about you.

Yours very truly, Mrs Vicar

Dear Michelene,

Told you I'd feel differently next time I wrote you. Building on your Mrs Noah idea – which I remain extremely dubious about for all the same reasons – I wondered, if you were so sold on some notion of the 'culturally symbolized mother', if I could offer you a vicar's wife as an adequate compensation for your 'mother in Israel' notion. (I made Sunday lunch last week for sixteen people three of whom were my legal family and six of whom were trainee clergy – five men and one woman. As we sat down to roast pork (!) someone called me a 'mother in Israel' and I am still confused as to whether this was a compliment or an insult.) I thought about a midwife or a headmistress of a primary school but sensed the wife thing was probably quite important to wherever your imagination was taking you. I realize that this may all too easily end up as an elaborate joke against myself, but there you are.

Let me know what you think.

Love, Sara

Dear Sara,

Thanks for your letter. Did I say I'd hurt my ankle? It was my knee that was sprained. When you dance, the knees take an awful lot of the strain, and lots of dancers have terrible trouble with cartilages and things like that.

The weather's been lovely down here, clear and very sharp, and I'm feeling a lot better, but I can't walk very far, so I haven't seen the Pavilion yet.

I hope you don't mind me writing back quick. I've never known a writer before, so I feel you are very understanding and wise. I think I'm mad all the time, and that it's only sheer luck that has stopped someone locking me up. When I was little my mother used to tell me I was mad and that if I didn't stop screaming she would get me taken away. Well, I think she used to say that, I can't remember for sure, and it isn't the sort of thing that people write down, is it? It could just be something that jumps up in your head and speaks to you and you don't know where it's come from or who it is.

There is a fly buzzing round this room, my friend Grace's study, where I'm sleeping and I hate it, it is a monster that is going to eat my eyes.

Please can I ask your advice? I have a friend. When I first met her, we were both at dance school together, and she was very lively and attractive, and not really a very good dancer but with bags of personality, and we used to have some quite good times together, and at the end of the year (she was in the first year and I was in the second year) we had a show and I persuaded the teacher to let her, her name was Grace, be in the show, which usually didn't happen, because you didn't usually have first years in second year shows. Then when I left college I joined up with a group, and when Grace finished I got Grace to join the group, and then I did a bit of choreography, and got Grace to help me. And then some funny things started happening. Grace started her own company and didn't ask me to be in it, and then she started choreographing things and they were terribly like what I had done, and then recently she has started doing solo spots, and they are also very like the way I dance. Now I get what jobs I can, I won't go into them, but the thing is that I am sure that Grace is persecuting me and I have dreams in which she walks behind me and puts her hands over my eyes and I can't see, and I have decided I am going to kill her. I want you to know this, because I think you will understand. Please don't tell anybody. I must stop this now because Grace has just come back and I don't want her to know I am using her typewriter.

From Frankie

PS (written later at night) Yes, I might let you see some of the diaries. I have one volume here, and the others are in different places where I have stayed.

Dear Frankie,

Thank you for your letter. I must have been muddled about the ankle. I have a wonderful strange friend who used to be a dancer and now she is in her seventies she has dreadful arthritis in her knees, so do please take care of yours because it makes her sad and depressed. She was the good witch of my childhood and from when I was about ten she made a space for me to be not like my family. She is the last of the Great Romantics and believes with a passion in illicit sex and the glories of Art. I think that is quite healthy for teenagers. Anyway, I'm wandering off a bit; except that I do think that having someone around who believes that you are a real artist does something good for the psyche. But what happens to those memories, I want to ask. When I contact my memories they are very seldom affirming, admiring, supportive ones. Perhaps that would be the final madness – to think that you were sane and everyone else was mad, instead of the other way round.

About Grace, since you ask; I don't understand why you are staying in her house. I think you should either kill her or move out. How will you kill her? Do you plan it in detail? I have never felt imaginatively able to kill anyone, only myself, and not that effectively. I'm sure I should be saying soothing things like I'm sure it's all in your head and of course she's not stealing away your dances and your ideas and your work. But I'm not sure, I'm not sure at all. I think there really are people that you cannot, must not, trust an inch, because they will steal everything they can get their hands on: I think that's why I was so defensive when you accused me of stealing from Françoise's diaries. I might be one of them and not know it. Something about being a feminist – I sort of expect that men will try and steal, appropriate, my energy and ideas; I don't like it but I have a sort of worn-down resignation about it, indeed sometimes I am fuelled by my own efforts to slip a quick one over on them. But when women do it it is different. I write a lot about women's aggression towards other women but I am always the victim of my own fantasies; so if you want, I will help you kill her, but we mustn't tell anyone. If you send me some more details, like how you would like it done, I will think of a scheme, because I am very good at plots (a nice *double entendre* there don't you think, coming from a writer).

If you liked, we could work out together how to kill her. Then we would discover if it was true that writing something means you don't have to do it, or if we still wanted to kill her. This would both be literary theory and useful – if you did decide to kill her in the end. If this notion attracts you why don't you send me lots of details about her and about how you would want it done, and we can play with them.

If, however, you have decided on all the salient points and don't want me messing about with your own murder, I should understand that. But you can't kill someone while you are living in their house and using – however secretively – their typewriter. Apart from the ethics too much suspicion would fall on you. (I'm assuming you want to get away with it (?).)

If you know when you're coming to London, let me know and we could arrange something. Because yes, I am willing to run some risks to see the diaries.

Take care of your knee and yourself, Sara

Dear Michelene and Sara,

I don't understand why you (or is it perhaps Sam?) are being so sticky about all this? Is there some problem I don't know about? Is there anything I can do to sort it all out so that we can all three get on with what I know we all want to do – write and publish your book which I'm absolutely sure will be exciting and successful?

Why don't the two of you come and have lunch with me and tell me all about it and see if we can't smooth out the pathways.

Yours, very enthusiastically, Nicky

Mrs Noah,

Fuck you frankly.

Of course we're in the garden and we're not coming back; no way. We've had to climb about three thousand sodding stairs (stairs are a clear example of the sort of speciesism we're complaining about) to get on to a typewriter to answer you. Luckily *they* were away for the weekend at a, guess what? A fucking heterosexual wedding. So we took our time: slowism is yet another complaint we've got by the way. The speeds write us out of culture, or mock us like that stupid hare; we're stereotyped all the bloody time. The only mention we get in *Roget's Thesaurus* is abusive – you know: tortoise = slowcoach. No mention of diversity; no mention of the beauty of wrinkled scaly neck-skin. Nothing. Sodding nothing. At least your boys are trying *slow*.

Anyway, what we want to say to you is that the whole project really stinks: do you have any idea how few species are into this humanist couplism: because of your own disgusting moralism you're planning to fuck up the sex life of about 94% of all species in the world. And anyway YOU AND HE HAVE MADE A RIGHT BALLS UP OF THE WHOLE THING FROM THE WORD GO. Why do you think the gerbils are sulking (bloody typical reformist liberals though they are)? Why do you think we've decided to opt out of mainstream culture altogether? We're DYKES sweetie, and don't you forget it. Wimmin and proud of it. You heterosexist creeps have only to see two happy tortoises climbing about on each other to come to fascist couplist conclusions.

So no we're not coming back. Look, it's hardly worth it; all we got out of the entire Old and New Testaments was one sodding reference, and you know what to? We bet you don't, no one bothers with tortoise cultural history. One reference, and that to say we're unclean – fucking dirtism, the Bible is full of it. And even that one has been written out as a mistranslation by these so-called scholarly modern translators; typical masculist, humanist elitism, it makes us sick. Lesbian tortoises have no fucking rights at all; you winge on about your oppression, well, sod you.

Count us out of your Brave New World. Let it sodding rain we say; we repudiate pro-sun anti-wet weatherism. Power to the antediluvian chelonian sisterhood. Power to all dykes with backbone – the more the better. Power to wimmin of all species.

Yours disrespectfully you sold-out wifist,
Armorelle and Gertrude

Dear Michelene,

Perhaps ideas are meant to be stolen or something.

I said I didn't want to do anything satirical, but it does seem to me that if you want to insist on a Mrs Noah theme (and you haven't yet responded to my letter properly) perhaps we could incorporate the animals and really have some fun???

I've just got Nicky's letter and presume you got it too?? Do you think it will do any good? If so I'm up for it. I'm broke and want to get this contract on the road as a matter of urgency.

Take care. Love, Sara

armorelle and gertrude,

well, now. lucky you that I found your letter. mrs noah is such a shloch, she may want to keep secrets but no way can she. basically, you should come back. basically, you're lucky I found your letter, because if one of the vertebrates had got it, or anyone but a small and hardly noticeable worm, you would be in shtuck. you have a very fundamental logical flaw in your argument, and that is that you are shooting off your mouths against couples, and you are absolutely conforming to all that's worst and defensive about the institution. running away, writing in a single voice between two, a lot of long words to cover up something very simple, which is fear. fear of being on your own, like I am, fear of facing the fact that it takes all sorts. right? I know you just look right over my head, you think I'm just a silly, slimy sort of thing, don't have your toughness, don't have your feelings, you think I hide because I'm stupid, you think anyone who doesn't look exactly like you doesn't exist, you really have learned to use your shell like some sort of grenade, and you've upset me. of course, you may just say fuck me as well as fuck mrs noah, but I thought you were my friends. I'm staying here, because this is my best chance of survival, and I think I am both of the world and different from it, and of course I'm jealous of your guts and courage but if you go on like this you're likely to fall down those unnatural stairs and crack your shell and then you will have gained nothing. if you don't want to come on the ark when this holocaust thing happens with the water, then you can at least come back till then. I won't say all is forgiven, because you've treated me like dirt, and I should know what dirt is, and I may forget, but I won't forgive, and it isn't just mrs noah you're getting at, it's the rest of us as well. The gerbils are of course ultra lefties, what else do you expect of them, spoilt bastards, they're not really reformists, they don't want anything to change, but I really thought better of you. actually, I tell you something, I started this letter feeling very upset, and prepared to promise anything if you came back. now I feel as if I'm crawling and begging and pleading and making a fool of myself, and fulfilling all your expectations of being a worm. so actually, over to you. if you want to take the risk of surviving in the cold, it's down to you. but I should warn you that mrs n is thinking of getting the law on to it.

winnie

Dear Winnie,

Don't be like that please.

You're probably hurt that we haven't answered before, but the typewriter has been locked up while the owners (sick) have been away on their bourgeois little foreign venture called holidays, and we can't manage those pentel things – we haven't got those nasty wriggly finger things (yeh, we know you'll say we're wrigglist but it isn't meant like that, honest) (and yeh, this is an admission of failure, does it make you feel better?).

So we've sat it out in the garden and considered the options, rapped a lot and really raised our consciousnesses and we're getting our heads together. We really did find all the sexist garbage going on *chez* Noah when we lit out pretty heavy and oppressive; we knew we shouldn't let them get to us, but it's really soft. We've thought about the options you know, this isn't just an adolescent caper. If we come back they're going to split us up; we know they are, send us to the/rapists. We don't know who's spying for the N's, but someone is – and we have our suspicions; that bloody pacifist dove for one, always sucking up and sacrificing herself (probably wants a big symbolic role, you wait and see, bet they give her a sex-change op. before they let her start representing spiritual powers and love-of-god and stuff). Look, all we really want to do is be together. But we are trying to do that in some sisterly way and you're right perhaps we do exclude other people. Of course we're scared, Winnie, we're scared as hell, and envious (look at the turtles, practically like us, but they can bloody swim around for forty days and forty nights and it may be tiring but they'll be around afterwards won't they?).

Look, tortoises are going to be totally excluded from culture; our contributions ripped off, our voices silenced and we'll be reduced to household pets and it doesn't look fun. Yes, there are problems with going undershell and lurking about in bushes. Political problems. But if we come out now they'll lock us up and take the law to us and god knows what all.

This letter is all about us. We think it was brave of you to write, but you can't expect us to come crawling back on our bellies writhing for mercy, and oozing around THEM. We need a broader-based strategy I suppose, but gay tortoises tend to get squashed in liberal alliances, no one really wants to focus on our problem. Still. There you are.

In sisterhood, Armorelle and Gertrude

armorelle and gertrude,

on the one hand you want special pleading for your gay and reptilian statuses, on the other, you shove your shells in everyone's faces, and tell us all to stuff it (you've got some good jokes) and then when crisis looms you're back to ask Daddy and Mummy for help – figuratively, of course, since I know you've never been really at ease about your parental origins, being bred specially for survival. To carry the flag of today into tomorrow on mrs noah's windy vehicle must feel as if you've been created merely for instrumental reasons, rather than from love, and believe me, I do sympathize. no one is suggesting that you have a future without one another. mrs noah, for all her franticness (you know, she hasn't washed her hair for two weeks, like the yak) has never said a word against the two of you. noah is full of prejudices, we all know that, but look at the difference between what he says and what he does. if he hadn't wanted you, he'd have thrown you out, noah is an empiricist (yes, I can reach for the vocab when needs be, just because I'm a non-vertebrate exile doesn't mean I can't hook into the culture when I want) and if he sees something works, he'll let it be. the only problem is, that you are very clearly indeed not working. I think actually that you're both spoiled and fucking greedy. You want the status of belonging, and you also want the flash of rebellion. I think you must swallow your pride and come back. everyone will be really pleased. I will be pleased. I miss you both, and miss our late night talks and then waking up next morning dry and bleary but feeling something important has been said. I can't come and see you because I've got some sort of acute depression, or anxiety. the black python says I've got existential angst, which comes from having no thick skin or shell at all, and makes me very vulnerable to taking on the sufferings of everyone else. I think that sounds a bit too religious for my liking, and even though I know the flood is inevitable, I know that it's to do with the ice caps melting faster than expected, and nothing at all supernatural. but I can't move very fast, and I think the journey across the gardens will be too much. I veer between missing you and being deeply hurt that you've abandoned me, because I always defend you to anyone who makes any snide remarks, and being angry because I think that you have so much more going for you than me, and that you just seem to want more and more while others have less and less. But I feel very bleary, so I don't know whether one feeling is any more dominant than the other. Maybe that's why I suffer, because I have to live with such conflicting feelings. Please come back. You've got me all muddled between upper and Lower case now.

Love, Winnie

Mrs Vicar,

Sorry. Not good enough. Not me, nor you. Me, I make the usual mistake of not finding out about someone else's ritual before making assumptions (ie, that you would be expecting someone not of your own people), then you take the interfering – yes, it was your word, and actually that's what it is – step of sending fucking social workers round. Other people don't understand your own habits. Just because I live in the middle of chaos doesn't mean I don't know where anything is (I know where EVERYTHING IS, which is more than you can say for Noah) and if any busybody, do-gooding, little middle-class girl with blonde permed hair comes anywhere near here she'll get an earful and an eyeful and you have really frightened me because the last thing I want to see is me and Noah carted off into care or something before we've finished our project. You can't imagine how much work there is to do, and I don't understand how you can all be so calm about it. Not only is there the Flood but the Thames barrier is going to be the joke of all time when it hits, and I intend to be absolutely ready. Not only that, but I have had a terribly upsetting letter from the sodding tortoises who are playing up with their silly games yet again. They know that we all accept them for what they are, but they have some chip on their shoulder (which they've made into a bloody great shell, so many chips, all of them have just melted together) and I really think you should stop giving them house room. I don't want to do this, but if you can't persuade them to come back I may have to ask the police – or at the very least a solicitor – to return them. They are under-age (infantile, emotionally and psychologically) and we are their legal guardians. Both had a very unhappy childhood and have been getting on very well here until they took it into their heads to run off. I still don't understand why. I hope it isn't any temptation at your end – your typewriter, perhaps, since I keep mine locked up. Please ring the social workers and tell them to lay off. Basically I am OK, not at all anti-social, just incredibly busy, and as you know I am not one who has many social graces. Badly brought up, you might say but then if Noah and me weren't slightly off the wall we wouldn't be seeing into the future enough to be getting the Ark together. We have got some wonderful bonding stuff which will finally solve the problem of polluted waters eating their way through the wood. Noah is doing a magnificent carving job on the cornices. Those bloody tortoises are just hedonists, when they should be putting their backs into it.

The plumber called, and was wonderful. Took a bit of manoeuvring to get her wheelchair up the ramp, but we managed. She likes the boat. By the way, when the Flood comes we may find we could do with some extra hands. You and the vicar may be welcome; but only if you call off the social workers and if Noah can be got to agree. If praying makes you feel good, be my guest. Me, I haven't got time. But my soul is in the right place.

Mrs Noah

My dear Mrs Noah,

You really must not upset yourself like this; I'm sure it cannot be good for your health or for poor Mr Noah's, who does not sound in very good form. I tried to come and visit you, because although I do hate the interfering clergy wife as much as you do I still think it is important to support one's husband's vocation – on that at least we do agree. But alas, it was rather difficult to approach your house as you seem to be engaged in rather extensive building works: I'm sure you're being careful not to overstretch yourself financially, you don't need me to tell you that worries about money do unsettle men dreadfully, and so often we wives have to be wise for them, don't we?

Anyway, to reassure you, my husband was very luckily among the civil dignitaries invited to meet Her Majesty at the opening ceremonies for the Thames Barrier (I do feel, don't you, that having a Christian presence on these occasions does add a certain dignity and charm), and the clever man who explained it all assured him that it would be effective in the very unlikely event of a major flood, completely, and he told me so; so I think we can trust God and sleep peacefully.

I am truly sorry about the social worker, I had no idea that she would be that type, so bureaucratic and officious. Really I think these sorts of things are handled better by the voluntary agencies, where the workers can only be motivated by real Christian charity, and interested neither in the money nor in the really rather silly ideas they are taught in colleges these days; I suppose I'm not really clever enough to understand all this modern sociology jargon, but quite honestly I don't think I want to.

Now, two little things; I am glad that the plumber worked out, she is a dear brave girl and I am very committed to the organization that trained her.

I am not sure why you think I have lured away your tortoises; apart from my absolute respect for family life, which I do think of as the basic glue of true Christian morality, I do try to keep my household running smoothly and I can tell you with complete certainty that two run-away tortoises would find no refuge here. As to the suggestion that they might be using my typewriter, well to be honest, that is ridiculous; I have brought my family up to have a true respect for privacy and personal property, we do not go about using each other's things – I mean since the children grew up; it has to be different when they're small, doesn't it, I mean nowadays a mother has to find out what they're doing so she can protect them. Anyway, your tortoises are not in my vicarage, and I should feel terribly hurt if you were to get either a lawyer or the police involved after this reassurance.

I do feel that you have a certain level of bottled up aggression, quite understandable given your trying home circumstances. I wonder if you would like to come to the co-counselling group we have here in the parish; or alternatively, our marriage enrichment courses, which my husband and I run so that people can gain help from seeing a truly Christian family love, in action.

About your boys. Would you like me to ask my very sweet friend who works in a cactus-leaf-addiction self-help group to visit them. I'm sure you would like her and she might provide you with an outside interest, which I do think is important, if you chose to get involved in her parents' support team.

It is kind of you to invite my husband and I to join you on a cruise; but I don't really think it would be quite suitable. Actually, this summer we are planning to look at early perpendicular churches in the Lake District. But I do, of course, appreciate the offer.

I shall try and call again next week.

Yours very sincerely, Mrs Vicar

Dear Mrs Vicar,

I'm sending over some home-made biscuits; pure butter, and with an almond on top of each. I hope you like almonds. I'm afraid you're wrong about the Flood and the Thames Barrier. Some years ago the Thames Barrier was breached by a freak hurricane in the English Channel – the most remarkable record of that is in a play called *Whores d'Oeuvres*,* written by a woman called Michelene Wandor. It's one of the few books I am taking with me when the Ark is ready.

I get regular reports from the stormy petrels, and yesterday we had an Ark meeting, to discuss the state of things with all the animals. The planks and bits and pieces you see outside are really the end of the work – everything else is more or less ready. I'll tell you now why I have been a bit off-putting about your coming over, and why I got so angry about the social worker. You see, the Ark is our house. I mean that the shell of the Ark follows the shape of the house on the inside. We decided that this was the best way to build it with the least amount of suspicion. It was Noah's idea really, though I helped with some of the minor details, for example I developed a new synthetic expandable resin, which on contact with the air will make our Ark as big as we need it for everyone. Of course, that isn't as important as all the sawing and welding and carving that Noah does, but I enjoyed pottering about with the chemicals and the test tubes in between hoovering up the woodshavings and making chicken soup. Of course it isn't real chicken soup (we couldn't, could we, with all the animals), it's just vegetables, but we still call it chicken soup. By the way, we have the most wonderful

* *Five Plays*, Michelene Wandor (Journeyman, 1984)

deep freeze, in which we estimate there is enough chicken soup to last until the Flood subsides.

Also, I'm glad you've got your Christian faith to keep you going. I suppose it's as good a belief as any, and I can see that it does make you and your family very happy. I wouldn't say we were HAPPY as a family, but I can tell you one thing, there's never a dull moment, and I suppose I like it that way. I love my boys, even when they are untidy and rude and loud and upset me, and you see, I would never need anyone from a cactus-addiction group, or any of that counselling stuff. You see, we have managed on our own for over 5,000 years.

And this brings me to the point of our letter. We are leaving next week. We were going to leave on Sunday (Sunday is really the first day of the week – in Hebrew, quite literally, the words for Sunday mean 'Day the First'), but Noah and the boys and the animals and I put a special 'Any Other Business' on our meeting agenda and we discussed all of you, and we have decided to ask you whether you and your husband and the children would like to come with us.

Let me explain first, we are prepared to leave on Monday (our 'Day Two') so that we do not transgress your Sabbath. We understand that you have your own ways, and we would not dream of trying to convert you or anything. We could agree between us that on the journey we would in fact have two days of rest each week, the Sabbath for us and the Sunday for you, and we think that would lead to mutual respect and alliance. I'm really anxious, because you have shown real friendship to us, and we think that in accordance with what you call 'Christian' principles, we should offer you the chance to survive. Let me assure you that I know FOR A FACT that the entire world will be destroyed. The reasons are very complicated, but it's really because things have got so out of hand that the only hope is to start afresh. In many places in the world the air is unbreathable; people give forth the fire of hatred and greed, competition rules and holds sway, so that even good friends regularly turn upon one another and pull rank. There can be no hope for a world such as this. I don't know why Noah and I and the boys have been chosen – we are far from an ideal family. But we feel we can make a further decision, and I think that it is very important to have another woman. I am not really very keen on having any more babies, and perhaps with you there – and of course your daughter for the future – we could share the load somewhat. It will be hard work, but I have read about your missionaries and you don't seem afraid of hard work.

Anyway, you can leave it till the last moment if you want. We have the space, so you can just turn up. If you want to bring any special food (wafers, that sort of thing) please do.

If you still decide not to come, then take care when the crisis comes; we shall be thinking of you.

Your neighbour, Mrs Noah

PS The tortoises are still absent and we are very worried. Winnie, our worm, is in a decline and is having to be fed on the purest mulch. I'd be grateful if you could keep an eye out for them. They're not steady on their feet, and I would hate to start out on such a long journey with an inhabited sick bay.

Dear Nicky,

I'm sending you this at home, since I have been dithering for what feels like days. We have various business things to sort out – such as Sara and Michelene's book, and the gorgeous Fraülein B – indeed, I do have the first part of the manuscript. It is a novel written entirely in letters between two characters, and I will let you have the MS as soon as I get the go-ahead from the German agent.

I gather you are to have lunch with M and S – I think that's the best thing. Between you and me, I think they would welcome some ideas for the book – just to get them going. If you're happy with the meeting, then let's get back to the contract.

This letter is about pleasure as well as business. Oh dear. I've probably said the wrong thing. Typical. What I mean is, where do we go after Frankfurt? I didn't expect everything to go quite so fast, get quite so out of hand, as it were, be quite so wonderful. Are we going to talk about it?

Love, Sam

Dear Sam,

Thank you for your letter; and for your promise to let me see this Fraülein B MS – frankly I shouldn't think it matters in the least what the contents are, do you? At least with her it isn't going to be all feminist theory and intellectualism, but I do take it kindly that you're letting me have a preview. Any chance of ducking the whole auction thing?

As for S and M (God, just noticed the initials, most unfortunate, we can do without that sort of joke), you know I'm willing to sign as soon as you can persuade them to accept the money as a best offer. At lunch they sat there stubbornly saying that they were not turning in a word until they had the contract and looking at each other to check every damn sentence with 'the collective'; I found it very irritating. I couldn't even get clear in my mind if they had the least idea what they wanted to do, or even if they've got a book for me at all; and yet they expressed great enthusiasm for the project in abstract – I tried to say that books didn't come in abstract, and fed some ideas: a humorous account of early feminist group meetings, presented as a sort of Canterbury Tales, for instance, women telling stories to each other with some bitchy gossip and wild amours to make the filler. 'That's interesting,' they said. I should tell you that I regard this book as my initiative and would be extremely peeved with them and you if you took it elsewhere.

Yours, Nicky

[handwritten]PS It is jolly hard to mix business and pleasure when you have a secretary typing your letters.

For goodness sake, Sam, you ought to know she will read the incoming ones first. Yes, we should talk about Frankfurt sometime; I thought it was surprising and wonderful too.

Take care. Love, etc, N

Dear Michelene and Sara,

I enjoyed our lunch immensely. I'm very excited about the idea of the book but will of course feel happier when the two of you get down to work and produce something concrete so that I can get our catalogue and publicity people working on it. I am sorry about the delays in producing the contract and understand why that worries you, but try to be patient, the contracts department wheels grind slow. I think you would probably find things easier if you worried less about it and left the small print to Sam who I can assure you has your interests at heart, and is fighting from your corner!

Let me know when you have some clear idea of what you want to do. I'm longing to see it.

Yours, Nicky

Dear Sara,

Have we arrived at an impasse before we've begun? The reason I thought of having a go at Mrs Noah (one of the reasons) was precisely because she seemed so far away from us; mythic, undervalued, more or less unknown, a 'Mrs', so that we could have some fun with her (this, remember, is before we decide who writes what) and generally get away from dull old social realism which I always feel we are pressurized to do. 'We' in a very general sense. I mean, I know that so much of your work has been mythically derived, and have great admiration for that myself, and where I have had a very minimal go at it have not felt in any way that I was 'taking' anyone else's characters. Indeed, I feel that Eve and Lilith are mine, because they are Jewish, and mine because they speak in my voices and mine because I wrote them. I would, of course, tolerate anyone else doing Eve and Lilith, but secretly I would feel (as you must with your Persephone *et al.*) that 'your' one is the closest to you and, therefore, the most *right* in a sense. I am not speaking of literary absolutes, but more of the way every writer/author MUST feel about their work. It is, yes, a kind of propriety, but one in which one says, yes, that is MY creation, I am responsible for it, and while I recognize that others may be doing similar things, or related things, I have no responsibility for what they do. I suppose I'm a bit puzzled by your response to my suggestion about Mrs Noah, because I find I hoped that the mythic aspect would appeal to you.

I have to confess that the idea of a Mrs Vicar figure makes me feel rather lost: a) because it feels too much like social realism, and b) because I don't know what she could be balanced with. I think that either we have to have two mythic figures or two 'real' figures, and not try and mix the two. I don't see what's wrong with you doing Mary Magdalene or someone like that. Couldn't we carry on the good old historic dualism and have a Jewish figure and a Christian figure, and see what happens?

By the way, I am NOT suggesting we start writing till the contract is done – so perhaps that is your paranoia about me being ahead of you – whatever that may mean.

As to what sort of fiction we could do – perhaps we should begin by listing what we don't want to do. I definitely don't want to write something that starts like: '*She closed the door with a sigh of relief, took off her coat and put down her shopping bag. The phone rang. She answered it.*' That is a sort of ploddy realism/naturalism which I like reading when it is well done, but absolutely LOATHE writing. What do you hate writing?

Michelene

Dear Michelene,

Have we arrived at an impasse?

What I felt was that we were at the tossing-ideas-around stage. Let me begin at the end of your letter and work upwards.

First, social realism. Well, you know my work a bit and you must know I have no enthusiasm for that and don't want to work with it any more than you do: though I suppose I am quite interested in muddling around the categories – you know – '*She closed the door with a sigh of relief, took off her coat and put down her shopping bag. The phone rang and her pet dragon answered it for her.*' I think this is called Magic Realism nowadays. And the reverse, if that's the right word – like your stunning story of all the housewives in the supermarket throwing the food around. Yes, I agree that social realism is, when well done, a delight to read, but it works best nowadays in detective stories which is another thing I don't want to write – something where everything else is dependent on the narrative events. Also, I don't want to write proper nineteenth-century well-rounded characters – mostly because the nineteenth-century novelists did it so well. And I don't want to write a clever-clever modernist book about the process of writing a book. And I've already said I don't want to write satire – though I would like to write funnier than I usually do, being so full of angst and drama; one of the things I most admire in you is that lightning shift of mood that you can do from one to the other.

This may not seem to leave us with much!! Except reclaiming the myths, which is I suppose what we're arguing about. Why *not* an Old Testament and a New Testament character?? It *looks* like a nicely balanced coupling, but for us as writers it isn't: your relationship to the Old Testament is a relationship to your cultural heritage – the equivalent for me is the Greek Mythologies and the Northern European fairy stories, not the New Testament, because as you know I am, really and truly, a Christian and Mary Magdalene is, for me, not a myth but a sister (of course, sisterhood may well be a myth, but it's not the same one). Suppose we did Eve and Mary – we would not be talking about parallels but differences; I couldn't make the same jokes, same connections as you can – not that I couldn't fictionalize around her, and I have done that too, but they wouldn't be matching fictions, and it would read very oddly. You say we can't have one myth figure and one real one – Mary is a real, not a myth figure for me. The matching fictions for us would be to take say Eve and Athena and we couldn't do that because they wouldn't match for the reader and anyway I'm having difficulties with the whole classical corpus now because so many people hear all references to it as elitist, but that's another story.

The idea of taking Mrs Vicar was about taking a contemporary myth (that sort of woman doesn't exist any more, thank God) and imbuing it with all the anachronism and wit and memory that is usually conferred on 'real' – read 'dead' – mythologies (well, not dead of course, still very much kicking, but readerish sort of people know they are myth figures, whereas they may not have identified contemporary myth-women as myths). How this could be seen as social realism boggles my mind – obviously I'm not talking about 'Tales from the Vicarage' but the sort of muddling of categories that I mentioned earlier in this now rather long letter. To use the privileged language of mythology to describe a cartoon character seems to me delightful – if I had had a better education in popular media I might well be proposing that we took a character like Olive Oyl, from *Popeye*, and used her.

Playing with myth is not 'rehabilitation' of the character and you know it.

Among the things I hate writing are letters like this where I feel I'm being forced into a fight not of my own making, and get defensive and aggressive both at once. This however is not an impasse, it is a search, or re-search if you want to be clever about it. I very much want to write this book with you for all the reasons we have discussed over the years, and I refuse to be put off. Of course there is a book here, somewhere, for us to write. We just have to find it.

Warm love, Sara

Dear Sr Mary Clare,

Many thanks for your hospitality the other evening. I really enjoyed doing the reading. Such a responsive group – with people laughing at all the jokes. Very perceptive of them! I particularly liked the feeling of having a clearly 'mixed' audience – right-on feminists, nuns and Jewish women laughing at (more or less) the same things. And the cakes and coffee were marvellous. I never bake myself, but enjoy other people's baking lots.

I hope I wasn't too harsh during the discussion; I mean the woman who asked me whether I had sold out because my work is published. I always get very angry when pious politicos attack writing as a profession, and heaven knows it's hard enough work doing it anyway and keeping earning a living without some dumb person attacking you for trying to earn a good living AND write the kinds of things you want to write. I always react sharply at that sort of question, because it is so double-binding. I've been asked it by feminist academics, who wouldn't dream of giving up their own jobs and living on air just because they are feminists, but somehow expect writers to be more moral or stupid, or more self-sacrificing than everyone else. The writer as martyr. Anyway, I'm beginning to sound off, so I'll stop.

Thanks, and I hope we'll meet again.

Yours, Michelene

Dear Michelene,

On the contrary it should have been me that wrote to thank you – and I expect/hope that you have heard, or soon will, formally from the committee. It was, I thought, a wonderful evening and though I shouldn't say so, the best we've had in the series so far: exactly what I hoped would happen, that meeting not just of intellects but of people. It was lucky for me that it did work because I had stuck my neck out an unsisterly long way (oh dear, the use of sisterly to mean nunnish is becoming increasingly difficult for me) in my conviction that we had to have some 'imaginative writing' as well as elegant theory and abstract theology.

Weren't the cakes good. It is an odd fact that nearly all nuns have a passion for sweet things: I have heard some extremely elaborate psychoanalytical explanations of a reductionist sort for this fact. If other feminists do too I shall feel less guilty about it in the future.

I didn't think you were unduly harsh during the discussion; but this may be because it is so entirely outside my experience (a commitment to voluntary poverty does seem to me a special grace; repaid in compensating factors like job security and no responsibility). Frankly, I thought the woman you argued with was trying to say something quite other – like she couldn't make a living by writing so why should you, as though her failure could be justified if the righteous were doomed to failure, therefore it was important to her that you should be proven unrighteous.

Actually the one bit of what you said that I wanted us to fight about – and I thought maybe a liberal fear of anti-semitism stopped people taking it up – was your comment that we (Christians) had appropriated the Old Testament, which seemed to me very strange and a-historical. No one, or even no one tradition, can own a text as enormous and complex as the Old Testament; it surely can be re-appropriated by anyone who wants to. But perhaps we could take this up some time. I would like to meet again if you would; it occurs to me that I know practically no one except you who isn't a Christian and that lets me say things to you that I can't say elsewhere. However, I'm in retreat at the moment (probably one of the reasons for this excessively verbose letter, silence goes to your head and there is almost too much God crashing around here).

I'll be back by the beginning of the month so that if you'd like some more cream cakes we could meet then?

With thanks for your charming and interesting reading.

Yours, Sr Mary Clare

Dear Sara,

God knows if you'll get this, it's such a godforsaken hole, godforsaken assuming that God ever got here in the first place, let alone created it, which I doubt, and I can't believe the object that passes for a fucking postman will ever get out of the pub for long enough to collect any letters from what laughingly passes for a postbox, more like a rusty pisspot, I say.

I've been in Australia for two months, working behind a bar, and may I say working a bit off-duty on the side, to be explicit, on the waste bit of the parking lot behind the pub, mainly I use an old mattress and thank goodness I'm strong from keeping up my dance exercises, and there are so few women worth looking at anyway that I'm not short of custom, but I've come down with some bug, probably the last lot of shearers who reeled through here on their way to see Ayers Rock and spent all their money so they had to go back to Perth with nothing but inflated beer guts and raging gonorrhoea. Anyway, I spent all my money on the doctor who is sometimes sober enough to be quite nice and he says I should lay off the game at least till I'm better: at least he didn't moralize at me, but I lost my job and I'm broke. I've got enough to keep me going till the end of the month if I sleep in the lean-to on the camel farm (I'll tell you about the camel trainer some other time) and I can live on scraps and bits and pieces, so if you could possibly send me a cheque for a hundred pounds, or better still, if you can send a money order for the amount in Australian dollars, I'd be really pleased and honestly it would just save my life. I wouldn't ask you only I'm at the end of my tether and I didn't know who to ask; people here just make jokes about finding a nice husband when I look for jobs, and I haven't even got enough money to get out of here and go somewhere else. I hope to be able to find work and earn enough money to come back to England but I have to get back on my feet properly first and get out of this choking dusty and dreary limbo. I don't know how anyone can think it's beautiful. It's all desert as far as I'm concerned.

Love, Frankie

Dear Frankie,

Bluntly – no I can't. Partly because I haven't got it. Even more bluntly, I'm annoyed that you should have asked. Final bluntness, what the hell are you doing in Australia anyway (unless you were fleeing the loathsome Grace and it seems a bit far to go in such a cause). Your letter is extremely confusing and has me slightly panicking, to be honest.

However, since it is horrid to be broke and miles away, and since apart from the camels, which sound intriguing, your plight does seem pretty grim, I rang up a woman I know slightly who has connections with a charity which was founded in the nineteenth century to assist repentant 'fallen women' and now has some difficulties in dispersing its funds. I had to lay it on a bit – your repentance, grief, etc – but if you're desperate enough to accept money from them you should get a cheque *post restante* Alice Springs in Australian Dollars, about the same time as you get this. I should warn you that the charity is a Roman Catholic one.

I still hope sometime to meet you and I am, despite it all, really genuinely interested in seeing the diaries. I hope things go better for you.

Take care and get well.

Love, Sara

Dear Ms Summers,

Please find enclosed a money order for £150 in Australian Dollars.

From the few details of your case which were put to me by Sara Maitland, I want to say that I can understand if the money sticks in your throat, but try to use it anyway, if you can bear to. If you need any other sort of help – cash or anything else – do let me know and we will see if anything can be done to assist. It is what we are here for. Formally, I would be very grateful if you could acknowledge receipt and even let us know a bit how you are – as this is pleasing to some of the older members of our committee.

I shall take the, I hope not too offensive, liberty of praying for you.

With best wishes, yours sincerely,
Sr Mary Clare, OSW
Hon. Sec.; The Maud Everton Charitable Trust.

Dear Sr Mary Clare,

I'm sorry to have taken so long to reply. I have been a bit hectic and preoccupied – and thought perhaps that if you were on your retreat, perhaps you wouldn't think me too rude for delaying my reply. I envy you having a structured way in which to retreat. I suppose in a way now I am in retreat – but in the odd comfort of my own home. I think I have a rather romantic idea of comfort and silence and freedom from the pesterings and persecutions (real and imagined) of the real world. Perhaps it is romantic because it doesn't take into account what you can face in silence. But it is a silence from the worldly horrors (both personal and nuclear, I may say) which retreat seems to promise.

I am really pleased that you like my poems. I think they're wonderful! And I don't say that about everything I write. But they are ME in a way that is quite rare, and that gives me pleasure. Interestingly, I am so sure of them that I am not bothered by the one or two horror responses I've got. For instance, I gave a copy to a man I know slightly – a very proper, 'straight' civil servant – and he said he found them interesting but didn't like them all, so I politely inquired for more detail and he said he found it very interesting about the two wives, how true it is that a man treats his mistress differently from the way he treats his wife. Well now. What was he trying to tell me, I wondered. That he had a mistress? That he would like one? Of course what it really meant was that he was simply reading the poems from within his own needs (oh, he prefaced the chat by saying, 'Forgive me for asking but are – are you Jewish?', to which I replied with an emphatic 'yes' and then watched 'cos he didn't quite know what to say back, as if he had said, 'Forgive me, but do you have syphillis. . . ?'). The other reaction which annoyed me was from a so-called Jewish feminist lesbian (rearrange the words in any order that pleases you best . . .) who was just plain bitchy and complained that the poems were not sufficiently Jewish, or feminist, or lesbian. Leaving all that aside, I felt I detected underneath a rather ill-written, unthinking review the fact that she was really complaining that I hadn't written her version, or her poem. Perhaps we all feel that, when we read things – at one level we are looking for a mirror to reassure, stroke ourselves, however objective, critical, culturally sophisticated we are.

On a personal note, the immediate impetus to writing *Gardens of Eden* was a voluntary rereading I undertook of the Old Testament. I began having very strong responses to it and began scribbling things which after a long time crystallized into the sequence you have. Now, after I finished reading the Old Testament, and before I began work on the material, I thought, well, I really should finish this thing and read the New Testament. You must understand that this is tantamount to breaking the most major taboo. When I was at school, at first I stayed out of Assembly because I was Jewish; then I felt left out and went into Assembly, but didn't join in with the prayers, and although I sang the hymns, I left out the words 'God' and 'He' and 'His', anything specific like that – ie 'Christ', 'Holy Ghost' – all that lot, because I felt that if I sang them I would be struck down, my betrayal would be noticed. And this from a confirmed teenage atheist.

When I read the New Testament I was shocked by two things. One that it is SO REPETITIVE (I do hope I'm not offending you) and I felt that my literary sensibilities were being hurt. (Of course this is irrational – there is nothing more fascinating than different versions of the same events, told from different points of view – this is, after all, what fiction is about.) Secondly, I got furious because I thought it was really anti-semitic and had the

NERVE to blame the Jews for what happened to Christ. I have to be honest and say that I am not terribly interested in any Christian *mea culpa*, *vis-à-vis* anti-semitism in the Church in the past. I think it is behaviour NOW that matters (I have this thing about ethics) and am, of course, also suspicious that this could be yet another way for Jewish experience to be suppressed and appropriated. But I say this also with other messages screaming in my head – well, I wrote a piece for Sara's book, *Walking on the Water*,* which expresses some of this conflicting feeling about being Jewish – and of course, anti-semitism in the end has to be overcome within the Church, just as Israel's political future will only become anti-racist when its internal political configurations begin to change.

I look forward to hearing from you.

Best wishes, Michelene.

* *Walking on the Water*, ed. J Garcia and S Maitland (Virago, 1983)

Dear Mrs Noah,

I feel dreadful, I feel truly dreadful. I got your letter, and the lovely biscuits (if everything turns out alright after all I hope you will bring some to the Mother's Union bring-and-buy winter sale, everyone would be so pleased) and first I ate them all and didn't keep any for the dear vicar or the children which was terrible of me; and then I read your letter and thought that you were mad or something and I had to keep my distance. Then the Monday you had planned to leave I woke up and it was pouring with rain, after the long hot summer, pouring and pouring. And I was frightened. And the vicar, who couldn't understand what I was on about, got quite annoyed with me. Of course, it did stop raining, as you know, and I see your house is still there; and without wanting to interfere I think you must do something about tidying up because the community neighbourhood group have been complaining. I said firmly that we could not interfere but they may take it higher up.

I'm afraid I'm rather dodging the issue. When I took our little spaniel for his walkies and saw that your house was still there I was so relieved: I realized it had been a warning to me. I have discussed it with the vicar – but I'm afraid he does not altogether understand, and feels that he ought in any case to stay with his people. I don't know, perhaps he's right; and if he does, perhaps I ought to stay with him – till death us do part and things. But in case he changes his mind, or I do something, I want to tell you that I am getting ready. I've sent my pearls to the cleaners – Mummy would be very cross, bless her, if I entered a new world with what she would have called 'shabby looking' pearls – and ordered four new twinsets and an extra pair of brogues.

I'm not sure, to be honest, some mornings I think I must be mad, or you, or both of us. And the vicar did point out to me the bit in the Bible where it says no more floods, but the rainbow comes and goes, doesn't it? I feel very muddled at the moment; I suppose what convinces me is that I was wrong about the tortoises. I have now reasons to believe that they may very well be lurking in the garden. If two tortoises of dubious moral standards can be hiding in my garden for several months without my knowing anything about it, then anything can happen. I'm afraid I was rather condescending towards you, but I will try to find them.

I really want to tell you, although I was very frightened by it, that I was terribly touched that you asked us to come with you. No one has asked me to do anything except because of my husband for years and years: vicars' wives, particularly if they're like me and not the bright young trendy sort, just get laughed at. You were kind to me and I had not been kind to you.

Please can you keep me up on developments. I don't think it was very kind of you to give me a false date like that, but I'm sure it was good for me and brought me to my senses; I often tell the children that sometimes one has to be cruel to be kind so I do try to understand. I will try to find this book by the woman with the funny name you gave. I have seen her name before but I thought she wrote things for the radio, I didn't know she did weather reports and things like that. It sounds most interesting, perhaps she would give a talk for the Young Wives programme this winter – and you could come and hear it.

God bless you, and thank you (and please do not tell anyone about this letter, because the vicar thinks I'm getting a bit funny and it makes him cross).

Mrs Vicar

Hey there, Mrs Vicar,

How about this for a game of sailors!

We are moored (well, that's a terrestrial term, but I mean we are static) off Margate so that we can do one or two little repairs – our solar panel which provides all the energy we need is proving to be less resistant to sea spray than we thought so we are working on a new coating.

We fooled you, eh? We went and none of you noticed at all. Remember I told you that I had been working on a compound which was infinitely (I mean literally) flexible – well, that meant that when we were ready to leave we simply folded the ENTIRE Ark up and slipped it out through the bathroom window into the side entrance so none of the neighbours would notice anything suspicious. And how did we and the animals get out, I hear you wondering? Well, that hole at the end of our front garden with the LEB van parked permanently outside – that was our exit tunnel. (The LEB van has no engine in it, you will find.) So we all snuck through that, wiped our feet, trundled the Ark down to the Thames and here we all are. So any mess you don't like outside what was once our house is all yours; clear it up, call the council, do what you want. Legally the house is still in mine and Noah's name (I made sure we got a joint mortgage) and if you're not angry with us for doing a moonlight flit, I wonder whether you'd mind keeping an eye on it for us. If you have any friends or know anyone who needs somewhere to stay, they're welcome to make use of it. Or perhaps you and the vicar would like to make use of it for prayer meetings, or nuns' tea parties or something. All I'd like to know is that it is being made good use of. It's probably a little silly, since you will all be engulfed sooner or later, but contrary to appearances I have a very practical mind, and don't like to see anything wasted that can be put to good use. (By the way, we'll probably be here for a few weeks yet, so if you would like to come and bring your pearls and twinsets, we've still kept a room for you all (on deck, so the view will be good).)

It also gives us a little more time to find the tortoises. Actually – would you like to come down here on a daytrip – without the vicar and your children, just you? You sound as if you could do with a bit of a holiday. Perhaps if you're not keen on the sea (I LOVE the sea myself) we could meet inland – somewhere, say, like Sissinghurst Castle. I think the lady who used to live there probably wore pearls and twinsets. She certainly did a lot of gardening and that seems to be a very nice English habit.

Anyway, do let me know. Letters are being forwarded to me from my previous address, so just send any reply there.

Best wishes and anchors away, my hearty – sorry about the euphoria; ozone always does this to me!

Mrs Noah

My dear Mrs Noah

Congratulations. I *do* think you are so clever and I *am* glad you are feeling more cheerful. It is probably the sea air which I think is always *bracing* after town life. I'm afraid that I could never have managed it, even to get off to the *shops* seems to be a *major* exercise for me by the time I have found my keys and rewritten my list and remembered what it was that I had forgotten to put on the list and *all* those sorts of things. I'm afraid I am not exactly what you would call *efficient* and it does make poor Mr Vicar so terribly cross and it is not as though I didn't try, but that is not the point. I *do* think it was clever of you to slip off silently like that though why you should have thought that I wouldn't notice I can't imagine and *in fact* I'm afraid that little remark *rather* hurt my feelings. However *of course* I will keep an eye on the house for you, though I can hardly let anyone in there at the moment because this very morning the LEB arrived to *investigate* – their rather unkind word – what they called the misappropriation of their van, even though I *explained* that there was no engine in it. In fact that seemed to make things worse not better although I *cannot* understand why and as it turned out we had a *few words* because I felt their whole *tone* was quite unnecessary. And then the police arrived, and as it turned out Mr Vicar had called them because from his study window he could not see that it was me who was talking to the LEB person but only that there was a bit of a rumpus going on and he thought it might be the beginning of a race riot – I do not know if I have mentioned to you that he has the most *terrible* trouble with his eyes and had forgotten to put his glasses on this morning – well he had not *forgotten* exactly – the truth is that he could not find them and since this was obviously my fault because I am so stupid and always losing *everything* he was not in a very calm mood. So then the police arrived in droves and *stormed* into your house and how I could ever think you had made a mess I cannot imagine because by the time they were finished with it; well, I tried to explain to them that they must not touch the china ornaments but I don't think it helped. But for the moment your house will not be very suitable for nuns' tea parties though it *is* kind of you to think of them and of course most nuns are Roman Catholic and I'm afraid their local priest, though I'm sure very sweet, has had words with Mr Vicar about whether Mary can be described as co-redemptrix so we are not on speaking terms at the moment. *Anyway*, I have had a simply brilliant idea and told the Girl Guides that the house has been made into a mess *deliberately* to help them with their badges and they are all working on housecraft and tidying it up and that nice plumber lady that I introduced you to came round to finish something off and she stayed to supervise the Guides and I was able to come back and find Mr Vicar's glasses for him so all's well that ends well as they say and I will of course keep a very close eye on your home because as you *know*, you can't trust anyone nowadays, though of course I trust *you*. I'm afraid this letter does not explain things very well and I have entirely forgotten to mention that despite the mess and everything I thought your house was *lovely* when I finally got inside and especially that your kitchen seemed terribly *sensibly* designed. I do think you are clever.

I would love to come for a visit and am certainly beginning to feel that I could do with a little break since I seem to be making a muddle of everything. And I still haven't explained my *ghastly* suspicions about the tortoises. But *no* time now or I will *miss* the post.

I am *very keen* on the sea, but also on lovely gardens like Sissinghurst and I do like to support the National Trust. I think they do *splendid* work, don't you, but so of course do the Lifeboats, so it's six of one and a dozen of the other or something like that.

I'll let you know when the Guides are finished and I can lock up your home in <u>safety</u>.

Yours, Mrs Vicar

Dear Sara,

Thanks for your letter. I don't believe you haven't got the money. But it doesn't matter anyway because that organization you mentioned sent me a cheque which arrived in the same post as your letter and it's saved my life and I've started to repay it.

I came to Australia because I got fed up. I got bored and picked up a shearer who was travelling by car across the desert to Alice. Anway, that seems like ages ago. I'm still stuck here – though I'm thinking of going across to Perth which is supposed to be very beautiful – forests, miles of lush beauty, etc – and it seems daft to have come all this way and not see the landscape.

Sometimes I don't know where I am or what I am saying. I don't know whether the diaries are real now or whether I just know them all in my head. I've been locked away a few times and I have all this stuff in my head and sometimes it comes out and I don't know where it's come from and other times I just feel miserable and nowhere. Maybe that's why I'm staying on here in Australia. Honestly, it is the biggest nowhere I have ever seen. I don't mind disappearing here because everyone else here has disappeared. They simply are not. I don't know what this means. You may not want to write to me again – you are the only person I'm writing to at the moment. My family are shits and Michelene just seems very unapproachable. Grace is dead and good riddance to bad rubbish.

I'm feeling very tired now and I must lie down because my head and shoulders are just too heavy.

Frankie

Dear Sr Mary Clare,

Thank you for the money. Considering I got chucked out of my convent school, I never thought a nun would be nice to me again. Are you *really* a nun?

Frankie Summers

Dear Frankie Summers,

I was glad to hear from you that you got the money. If it is any comfort to you I got chucked out of convent school too once but despite that I really am a nun. And probably because I am a nun I am allowed to ask, though you are not obliged to answer, if you really are alright?

You should bear in mind that it was not as a nun that I was 'nice to you' but because a faintly silly old lady left an enormous sum of money and asked the Church to administer it as a charitable trust. My Order were privileged to get the job and one of us always is secretary to the committee; but it is the committee that gave you the money, and they gave it because they have a legal obligation to do so – there is no need to be so grateful, honestly.

Nonetheless, I do think it would make them happy if you felt like writing some sort of letter explaining your circumstances and particularly in what ways you decided to use the money: if you feel they were nice to you, it would be very nice to them if you could. They mean well.

It is raining gently here and although the garden is consequently looking wonderful and flowery, I can't help envying you your great open desert and a bit of sun; so I hope your health has improved and you are enjoying it.

With best wishes, Sr Mary Clare

Dear Mary Clare,

I'm glad even respectable people like you were chucked out of school.

Yes, it's only fair that you should know a little more about me, as your Order has been so generous.

I am a writer, and I came out to Australia to research a thirteen-part television series about the history of women in Australia. It is being co-produced by Channel 4, a German television company and the Australian Broadcasting Company, so it is a fairly heavy responsibility. I also thought it would be a marvellous chance for me to finish my fourth novel out here. Don't worry if you haven't heard of me – I write under a pseudonym because my stuff is so autobiographical that it may upset my family. My first novel was about my first child – a very difficult birth and the child was deformed. Fortunately, it only lived for a short while. I kept very detailed diaries of it and based a novel on it all. So you can see that it is important to me to protect my family. I am sure you won't tell anyone about it.

I needed the money because my bag was stolen and I simply couldn't get money quickly enough from the TV companies. But everything should be alright now, and the cheque helped me over a very bad patch.

Thanks again for your help.

Yours, Frankie

Dear Winnie,

Look, we're sorry you're not feeling too good, but that's hardly our fault. We asked you round to talk because we wanted to have a chance to show you that we're right, that's all. Don't moan to us about 'conflicts' when they're self-inflicted: if you won't (can't, daren't) wriggle away from your own environment and conditioning, that's not our fault. Token animals make us spew. Look, they just want to use you. As we see it from here, radical animalism, a complete withdrawal from masculist, anthropist culture is our only hope. And so what if there won't be any future: better dead than red, so to speak. And long live the Kamikaze crews.

This is not romanticism, it is a political analysis. Right now we've got it made: this is as near paradise as any post-lapsarian reptile is likely to find – so long as we don't eat any of the fruit from the trees that the vicar and his simpering missus will notice.

None of this is our fault. The text says quite clearly, 'The wickedness of man was great in the earth and every imagination of his heart was only evil' – well, speaking as feminist animalists it ain't our problem and we're not going to wear our shells thin at the edges trying to help Them out.

Here we daily celebrate our powers, lumbering by the light of the Moon Turtle – the great One who shelters us under her shell (extraordinary that an anthropoid – of either sex – has never really looked at the meaning of their vocabulary).

So we'll all die, but we at least will die free and independent, needing no one, wanting no one.

Come and join us. We would welcome you as we will welcome anyone who is prepared to come. All history is human history. All culture is human culture. Fuck the lot of them, we say.

Come on, face the political realities and stop squirming about.

Armorelle and Gertrude

Dear Armorelle and Gertrude,

I really feel very bad, but there isn't any option. We have already left and so even if you were to change your mind or minds – no, mind is right – you seem so stuck on being parrot images of one another – no offence meant to the parrots, dear squawkers that they are – it is too late. I miss you both terribly, but if you really are hell-bent on ostrich-like (no offence to the ostriches, melancholy dreamers that they are) self-annihilation, there is nothing I or anyone else can do. I would just leave you with the thought that you have espoused the most reactionary of radical philosophies; you have taken on a blinkered ultra-leftism which is so way over to the left that it comes round full circle to the right. Basically, you are more interested in the destruction of everything than on its survival for a better and braver future. I know this comes from your contradictory combination of an impenetrable shell and a desperately sensitive underbelly, but frankly, when it comes to you or me – ie, which of us is going to survive – then I have to say fuck you and whatever radical animalism you espouse. You are indeed on your own, and I suspect that if you were here you would probably roll over on top of me, crush me and then think it was all my own fault. I'm not playing those games any more – and wouldn't even if we were still just down the road. Call me a crypto-copout, or a closet social democrat, but I still would like to live in a world where people will take responsibility for their own power. And really, you are just not.

So I'm miserable, because I feel even more lonely than usual without your cabbage-imbibing presences to heat the air.

Love, Winnie

Dear Winnie,

I passed, in the soft and windy silence of the night, through the garden where the tortoises dwell; there was a dulcet purity and I felt that I moved in the eternity where the masculine and the feminine are as one, cosmic images of fullness, and in that vision/dream I saw you and your struggle for wholeness and Being. They, poor lost ones, sunk in the mire, cannot participate in holy dreaming, but we, from different ends of the spectrum of beauty which embraces all things, can and must.

Since I feel, for myself alone, that money is the bane of civilization I am going to have to pop this little scribble into the slightly mud-soiled envelope of those two sad souls. Since they have asked me to post it for them this will not be hard. You cannot write to me for I am an ethereal now, and range the hills of dreamtime, but my heart goes out to you and greets you with a kiss from the hem of the shadow of the everlasting.

Sincerely yours, Eustacia-Rose Unicorn

Darling Eustacia-Rose,

How beautiful of you to write to me. I am so glad that you are watching over the tortoises, even though you see so clearly how short-sighted they are. They have found a whole lot of long words and I think they're drunk on playing truant. I don't know whether I'm more hurt at them for abandoning me, or more worried about how they will manage when they realise what a risk they are taking. More hurt probably.

I know I can't send this letter to you, so I am just thinking the words very hard and I'm sitting on the deck of the Ark, looking up into the sky. It is very clear tonight, just a few little wispy clouds against the dark blue sky. The moon is full and there is a shadow across it. I like to think that it is you – going anywhere you please, playing with the stars, running round the edges of the black holes of the universe and kicking stardust over the edges. I know there is a world where the masculine and feminine (or should it be male and female) are one, but it is so hard having to live out as an unproblematic (that's a long word I learned from Armorelle) reality what for other humans and animals is terribly problematic. I do not have to make these choices, and yet I can't be happy because I am alone in my non-problem. Do you find the same? Is there somewhere – in dreamtime, or in mindspace – where we can just smile at each other?

Please think towards me.

Your earthbound friend, Winnie

My dear Mrs Noah

I *just* thought I should drop you a *line* and let you know that your house is now *perfectly* safe – or at least the downstairs is and I have no *particular* reason to worry about the *upstairs*. I just hope you won't feel that I have taken *too much* of a liberty. The plumber is now living there, on a part-time, caretaker basis *of course*; she was in *real* need and I thought a much more suitable person than some nuns. She is terribly nice and *nearly* as clever as you are and I'm sure will take care of everything, and then *either* the Flood will come so it won't matter or you will return and *all will be well*. I did *try* and explain about the expandable resin and getting air bags for her chair, but she gave me a *very* fishy look so I think she will be alright in any case. Mr Vicar thinks I have *exceeded* my responsibilities and he is probably right but I couldn't quite *explain* to him how it was that I knew you would not mind about the house as he also gave me rather a peculiar look and suggested that I went to see Dr Burns, our *wonderful* GP: I was quite *touched* that he should have noticed my rash because it isn't very obvious and I don't think men are very observant usually, but when I tried to *explain* this to him he looked *stressed* and said he did not mean that and perhaps he would go and see Dr Burns first, which of course I said would be *quite* unnecessary. But *anyway* I thought you would probably want to know that the house *was* safe and you would *not* have to worry about it any more.

Love from Mrs Vicar

PS Oh dear, I have forgotten *again* to explain to you about my suspicions about those tortoises. I may be unfair because I have no direct *evidence* and I don't want to accuse anyone, even a tortoise unfairly, but there is not time *now* because the Ladies Knitting Circle is just about to meet and I must make them all some tea; I wish I could bake biscuits like *yours*.

Dear Frankie,

I'm honestly glad that the money came through and that things are a bit better for you.

I was angry, and I think you might/ought to know why, but it doesn't matter. I thought I wouldn't write again at one point, but I am and it's probably mostly curiosity (an important part of my make-up which has got me into lots of trouble and also some good places). I'm curious about lots of things – firstly the camels??? More seriously, about the diaries and how things get in and out of our heads. And also something else, which you may not want to explain and certainly don't have to. Last week I went to Folkestone to do a writers' workshop thing. I got talking to some of the women over lunch and one of them (blonde, middle-class soft-punk style, rather tall) was called Grace and by some complicated process it turned out that this woman was a friend of yours. She asked after you quite tenderly, but since I had plotted her death with you – at least imaginatively – I found it a bit difficult to respond to her, and I did not tell her where you were. Actually, since you said in your last letter that she already *was* dead, I thought that either this must be a different Grace – or you'd been misinformed – or you'd made it up for some reason. Which is it? I'm curious.

I'm sorry that life seems muddling. I've always longed to go and spend time in a desert, so your experience is discouraging. Historically/spiritually, deserts are the place for both temptations and revelations. Why don't you try recording them – making diaries of your own. (That sounds aunt-like, but again I think it is curiosity.)

Take care of yourself anyway and do write again if you want to.

Best wishes, Sara

Dear Sara,

I don't know when I may come back. I have fallen in love with a woman who looks like a camel. I mean, she is tall, imperious, has bright red hair, a nose that points ahead, and is strong and stubborn. She is working here on a community project and she and I go riding on camels into the desert every evening. No, a desert is not a place to spend time in unless that is all there is left.

Yours, Frankie

Dear Nicky,

Sorry about the delay in replying. I have been snowed under.

Business first: glad that M and S (I prefer thinking of them as a business partnership, you see, rather than a taboo feminist fantasy) seem to be getting down to things. I am sure they will take all your suggestions very seriously. Though between you and me, if we are trying to hatch a genuinely commercial project, haven't we had enough of these interminably worthy women's-group novels – you know, the sort of lying thing where women 'tell stories', pretending that they're all sisters and lovey dovey. You and I know that women are as fickle towards one another as men; and their loyalties are based on useful alliances rather than goodwill abstractions, just like everyone else's. I hope you are not going to push them into some sort of formula fiction. After all, their great strength is that they both have scatty and rather dangerous imaginations, and with a bit of luck they can produce something quite daring together. This is, of course, between you and me, since I will support whatever they decide to do. I am working on your offer with them. I find the best way is to be silent for days, so that the wearing down process is gradual; basically I don't think you should offer any more. Just give me a little time.

Still business: I am sending this to you at home (AGAIN) precisely because I would prefer your secretary not to see it. I get the sense that you would rather not refer to Frankfurt again. So be it. It will not stop us doing business. But it will stop me assuming I can get anything very straight from you. I should have known better. But I have always been something of a secret romantic. Why I became an agent, I'll never know. Yes,

I do. I became an agent because I am good at negotiating. I like the money, the lifestyle, the parties and the travelling. And the occasional surprise – such as Frankfurt.

That's it. Show it to your secretary if you like. I'm sure she knows far more about you than I do anyway.

I'll come back to you on M and S.

Sam

Dear Sam,

Since I know that you are a very good agent – more than just a good negotiator, so stuff that false humility – I cannot make head or tail of a remark like, 'I don't think you should offer them any more.' If you mean you are sure I won't and want to be on the winning side, say so: you are always on the winning side from my point of view: apart from anything else you represent some of the best writers in the business and you can always get your hands on things before the rest of us even know they're there to be got.

And I would be more than happy to discuss Frankfurt, just not in letters on my secretary's desk. I have left you several messages on your answering machine, after all. Let's have a drink one day next week, get this M & S (thank you for that) contract tied down and discuss Frankfurt, etc, for hours. Groucho Club or somewhere more *intime*?!!! Thus mixing pleasure and business as in the good old days. But don't be grouchy (poor joke).

Love, Nicky

Dear Nicky,

God, you are a pompous ass. I mean between you and me, that if you stick to your offer, M and S will in time accept it. Frankly, they are not authors I expect to yield an awful lot on my investment – though I still believe this book will be commercial on its own terms. I think the gorgeous Fraülein B has far more going for her, given that she touches the edges of pornography and eroticism. I should, of course, not have encroached on your bargaining position. I was momentarily unprofessional. I suppose that is what comes of mixing business with pleasure.

A drink – fine. The Groucho – fine. Then, if we want to proceed to the Gay Hussar, we can do so. They always keep me a table on Fridays. 6.30 do you? Look forward –

Best, Sam

Dear Michelene,

I found your letter quite troubling, to be honest. I'm glad you waited until I got back from St Lioba's, where I was having quite a hard time with my retreat. Troubling because it is difficult for me to evaluate (for myself) much of what you're saying: in the first place I simply don't know – or at any rate, don't know that I know – any Jewish Lesbian Feminists. (There are some Roman Catholic Lesbians actually.) It may seem dreadful to say this, but in a way it is something that is tabboo in convents – I mean talking about it. This is probably because we're accused of it so much, and also because there is an inevitable element of truth in those accusations – women who join religious orders must at least like getting most of their emotional succour from other women. But I fear that you and I may have so widely different a cultural experience that anything I say about either your writing, or the biblical texts themselves, may be in a foreign tongue.

To match your 'personal note' I must tell you that, brought up as a Roman Catholic (and mainly educated in RC schools), I had exactly the same reaction during four terms that I spent in a non-parochial school. Like you I left out all the specific words about God because I thought that to use them in a Protestant Assembly would be an act of betrayal – you probably find this completely baffling.

About the New Testament. Your response is fascinating, because while you find it repetitious, most Christians find it frustratingly un-repetitious: this is supposed to be the authorization of our faith and the Gospel writers can't even agree which day of the week the crucifixion took place! The whole thing is shot through with contradictions. If you find the Gospels anti-semitic you should try Matthew who, although he appropriates the prophets for what you would see as his own use, is deeply concerned to claim Christianity as part of Judaism and lay all the 'blame' on the gentile imperialists – the Romans. Which does not, I admit, let us off the hook. But I will not breast-beat if that is not useful; I agree that present action is what is relevant, but how should we act? Part of what I'm asking, I think, is about you being so definitively Jewish (definitively in your terms, from what you said about that man who asked you), but not having the religious bit. I suppose you will say – and rightly – that a person can be Spanish or Polish without being a Catholic; but to a gentile (is that right, or is non-Jew better?), Jewish nationhood and Jewish religion seem very tightly interwoven – or is that too a product of anti-semitism. I do hope this is not just vague curiosity: being a biblicist has to mean attempting to enter into the experience of the text which does indeed include the Old Testament.

Oh dear, I do seem to rabbit on rather, I am sorry. I also want to ask you lots of other things too – like how you respond to Liberation Theology and also what you mean about fiction being different versions of the same event, which also sounds quite theological although it may not be at all. If you'd still like to meet for coffee, Tuesdays are my day off and I could easily come over to Swiss Cottage any time you like. Is the 30th or the 6th any good? At say, about 3.30?

And no, your letter did not seem off the point at all to me.

Yours, Sr Mary Clare

Dear Sr Mary Clare,

How very interesting to hear that you had the same experience towards the C of E God, as a Catholic; I suppose for someone who is Jewish, a Christian is a Christian – there is a sort of reverse snobbery about it – and it is silly, really; but I must say that, as I have allowed myself to become interested in aspects of Christianity, it is High Church or aspects of Catholicism which interest me – but I'm aware that at the moment I couldn't easily back any of that up. Perhaps it's just that in getting to know Sara and her husband I have felt there were quite surprising points of contact, so that I could translate that contact back into thinking that at times they could be 'almost Jewish'.

Perhaps we should sort some categories. No, Jewish nationhood and Jewish religion, and cultural Judaism (or Jewish culture) are all different things, which may or may not be related to one another. But you cannot deduce any of the others from the one. Just as, I suppose, you can be brought up in a Christian State, but not have any religious belief or practice, and nevertheless be stamped with its values, its associations, etc.

My Jewishness is not something I have (until now) emblazoned as a characteristic. I have been far more concerned, to date, to build on being a feminist and a socialist. I would like to try and explain this face to face – a letter seems to ask for complete paragraphs, sentences that are worked out, and I don't want to say things that sound like a formulated definition. I also want to ask you about Liberation Theology, about which I know nothing – but I am formally very untaught in most things, despite having the tail end of an elite education.

Yours, Michelene

My dear Mrs Noah,

I've *got* the tortoises and I *am* coming. I'm afraid it may take a while because I have to walk; I couldn't *really* bring the car because the vicar had to go to Deanery Synod.

I think I had better explain a bit. Two weeks ago I had to take the Youth Group on their outing, and it turned out that they were going to visit the Thames Barrier – *what* a coincidence! Somehow, I had always imagined that it would be a decent strong dam. But when I *saw* it the only thing I could think of was that *dreadful* Sydney Opera House. As soon as I actually *saw* the thing I realized that *everything* you had said was *absolutely* true. I must admit this was a *bit* of a shock. When I got back to the vicarage I tried to explain it all to the vicar but I'm afraid he was rather peevish about it all and said I was being silly and supper was late. He had had a very *tiring* day, because with me off with the Youth Group he had to get his own lunch and answer the door-bell. But he was rather extreme about it and I got quite *upset*. In the night I couldn't sleep so I went into the garden: I know this sounds a *bit* odd, but recently I *think* I saw a unicorn in our garden and I feel that I must check this out. *Anyway*, I went into the garden and to my complete surprise there *were* the tortoises – I'm afraid I *can't* tell you what they were doing; in all my years here I have *never* seen anything like it in a vicarage garden. I don't quite know what to make of what happened next. *Partly* being cross with the vicar, *partly* being so muddled about everything, and *partly* the realization that there was *something* I could do for you, after you have been so kind to me, I *pounced* on them – I'm afraid they do not have very nice natures;

the smaller one bit me quite hard on the thumb – popped them into a cardboard box (I always keep cardboard boxes when I get them – you never know when they may come in handy) and made off into the night. I started walking towards Margate, although I don't have a very good sense of direction. Luckily I always wear my pearls at night (Mummy always said it gave them a healthy glow – the warmth and the natural body oils) so I have been able to pawn a few for money. And I sensibly pulled on a pair of stout brogues – it does always pay to buy good quality shoes. So I am doing quite well, but not making very fast progress; this is partly because if people see a woman wearing a flannel nightie, brogues and pearls and carrying a cardboard box you do get some funny looks, so I try to go by the by-ways and mostly at night. But also I keep getting distracted; I think the vicar would call it lost, but between you and me and these four walls I am having the time of my life. I keep meeting very interesting people.

I certainly do like the sea, and I am a surprisingly good sailor. This always makes the vicar very cross as he gets sick as a dog at the sight of a wave, and I'm afraid I always find this rather funny which is cruel of me, but I can't help it.

I'm glad you are euphoric, and I'm most impressed by your creativity and the business with the LEB van. I'm afraid all I can do is knit.

With many, many thanks and I will take good care of the tortoises.

Mrs Vicar

Dear Mrs Vicar,

Hurray, hurray, hip hip hurray, you can't see me but I am jumping up and down in my Fair Isle socks because I'm so pleased that you're coming and that's why my writing is all wriggly – but I am so pleased, you can't imagine. What I was dreading most was being – not only the only woman – but the only mature woman on the ark. (There, you've got me at the underlining, but I think that's a sign that there's a lot I can learn from you.) Now; there is so much, I don't know where to start, so perhaps I will just go through your letter to make sure I answer everything. First of all, you are probably wondering how this letter reached you. Well, the barn owl gets very restless here at night, so I suggested to her that she could keep a look-out for you on your way here and deliver the note to you. If you want to reply you can just leave your answer where you found this one and Tawny will bring it back.

Right. Where was I? Well – forget about the Thames Barrier. No good at all for what we're facing.

Thank you so much for bringing the tortoises. No doubt they will sulk their little heads off, but it's winter anyway and time for them to hibernate – perhaps they were being a bit sluggish anyway and that's why you found them. But I think they have to have a cooling-off time to get over their rebellion and then they will be very useful members of the community next spring. We all look forward to having them back, especially the sea turtles who have gone right off their fish.

Now, you must be very careful – I think you will probably feel very homesick for the vicar. Perhaps we can find a way for you to keep in touch with him, or even for him to join us on a later leg of the journey. I don't know how long it will take you to get here, but we'll wait till you arrive – Tawny will keep an eye out for you, and I hope you don't catch a cold just in your flannel nightie. I hope you have some warm underwear with you at least – we have a good stock of Damart here on board, so you can share it when you get here. By the way, I should warn you: Noah and I chat a lot in classical Hebrew, with bits of Aramaic thrown in; we find it very soothing when we're doing the washing up or mixing the pigswill (you can imagine what a dilemma it was over the pigs, we had the most terrible row while we were trying to decide whether to bring them with us or not – I started off being against and Noah for, and we argued so much (in Aramaic, and then Yiddish a bit) until we switched positions and then I was for and Noah against, and in the end we just burst out laughing). Please don't pawn all your pearls. Noah's mother gave me a double strand as a wedding present, but they were burgled during the riots following the sacking of the Second Temple. As you can imagine, the police were totally unreliable at that time, so I didn't even report it. But I loved holding them in my hand, and I'm sure pearls suit you. Have you brought a twinset with you? I have just finished carding the wool from the last sheep shearing, and am dying it with vegetable dye and then I'll get knitting. If there's enough, I could do one for you too.

Let me know – and give the tortoises my love and tell them we won't be angry, and that I am reading lots of revolutionary literature so we can try and understand their point of view. By the way – I hope you don't mind me saying, but if you have any tortoiseshell combs or anything, it would be most tactful of you to hide them for the moment. . . .

Yours, Mrs Noah

Dear Winnie,

We'd like to continue with your political education, but right now we're really buggered up. We've been tortnapped, not merely by a bourgeois liberal humanist, but one who appears to be completely round the bend. (Look, sorry, nothing meant personally about curved and flexible physiques.) We can't write properly because we're cooped up in the dark being tortured by sensory deprivation.

It's making us think a bit, though. I mean we were going on about individual freedom and utopian concepts of that sort, choice. Choice. We seem to have overlooked historical inevitability. We think this crazed old maternalistic imperialist fascist may be bringing us – forcing us – onto the Ark after all, and what can we do? Sweet f.a., that's what. Fuck it. We also didn't fully recognize the power of sizism – she's just bloody bigger than us.

We're not sure what's going on, or how to formulate a proper political offensive, because we're in the dark as to the historical context – along with everything else.

If you can pick up any clues, please let us know.

In sisterhood, Armorelle and Gertrude

Dear Sara,

I love the idea of a magic dragon. We seem to be agreeing on at least something. Are we talking about writing a children's book? Don't tell Nicky and Sam; they'd have a fit. I totally agree; no clever-clever modernist (or should it be trendy post-modernist?) rubbish about writing a book about writing a book. Frankly, the English can't do it. They're just self-conscious when they try. I would actually love to write a massive nineteenth-century novel because it is the thing furthest away from me and the thing I can do least. I suspect that what I'm actually best at is precisely what, in others, I would dismiss as trendy modernism. But then, I think it is most difficult to appreciate people who write like you. Perhaps that is why I am drawn to the myth business, with which you seem so comfortable.

But problem: I don't want to take Eve again. I've 'done' her a bit, and if I did her again, I think I would want to control her voice completely. However, I am drawn to the balancing of Eve and Mary. Even, I have to admit, if I feel rather proprietorial about poor old Mary too. Though I am afraid they are still both myths for me. I think there's something in the idea, though I'm not clear what. Of course playing with myth is rehabilitating the character. It is a wave of the wand, a bringing to life of a figure everyone knows and precisely because everyone knows (or thinks they know), one can do what one wants with her. She is safe, and she will survive anything and everything. That is why the myth always belongs completely to the writer, and why the writer has absolutely no responsibility towards her. That is why I envy you your ease with the classics. And frankly, just 'cos some stupid sod says it's elitist, you and I know that isn't going to stop you retelling a story when you have something to say and do with it.

What does slightly puzzle me is the tone at the end of your letter. Am I forcing you into a fight? And about what? We both agree that we want to write this book, we both agree that we shan't put pen to paper until the contract is signed and I thought we both agreed we should discuss it the while. Are you hinting now that you are not sure about wanting to write the book? I don't think we can simply 'find' the book. Writing isn't magic, it's fucking awful, hard work. Are you saying I am being aggressive? You KNOW what I'm like – though it has to be said, you only know about the battles I have fought from my accounts of them. You have never actually been present. I hope that, if we have any conflict of views, we can produce a creative fiction out of it. And until the contract is signed and we have a really serious meeting about it all – let's continue to fling things at each other in letters.

I have to say, by the way, that we were brilliant with Nicky; every time we received or parried a suggestion, we must have appeared absolutely united and sure about what we were going to do. Of course we are absolutely sure that we can do it, but publishers never believe that of writers. They think we are shy, rather stupid flowers who only come into bloom at their bidding. The cynic is visiting today instead of the muse. I must show her the door.

Where next?

Love, Michelene

Dear Michelene,

You're right and I was being disagreeable. We artists do tend to be shy and stupid flowers, prone to attacks of weevil, blight and paranoia. I'll match you a magic dragon for a magic weevil any day of the week; and if Nicky and Sam want to call it a children's book, let them.

To be honest I am getting fed up with the whole thing and it winds me up. I really want it to work – I mean our book – and I'm getting to the 'touch wood' superstitious phase about it now. I agree we were ace with Nicky, but it was an impressive bluff. I'm not saying you are being aggressive, I am saying we are having great difficulty getting together a contract for a book whose most basic subject matter we don't even have formulated. And that this is good, not bad, but dicey – or feels that way to me. I mean – of course I don't expect to 'find' the book magically, but I think we'll only find it by bumping around quite fiercely, a process which I, for one, am certainly finding hard work. BUT I AM NOT HINTING, AND DO NOT EVEN CONSIDER, THAT I DON'T WANT TO WRITE THE BOOK and I'm both sorry and worried if my tone in the last implied any such thing.

So back to throwing ideas around. Would you really like to write a great big nineteenth-century realist novel? I'm amazed. But you could if you wanted to, I suspect: something to do with an innate grasp of sense of direction or form that you have, so that you seem to understand what it is you are doing, and even more what it is you have done.

About the classical canon, I think you're a bit simplistic. Yes, I seem to find myself at home there, but I don't want to tell the stories, I want to use them – I'm a terrible moralist at heart – and if people can't read/hear them for whatever reason, then you have to go and look somewhere else. Or of course assert such authority that they have to enjoy themselves. I think I did that innocently at one point, and now I can't any more; the question is whether I can do it craftily. Anyway, this isn't really to the point: Eve and Mary – could we allow each other, do you think, could you allow me to play Eve who is both your culture and a character you have already worked with? I think I would have a hard time allowing you a Mary, not just because I've fictionalized with her occasionally – as in *Daughter of Jerusalem*,* for example – but because of the massive emotional withdrawal it would involve for me, just detaching myself the right distance to have some image that is important to so much of my life in a book partly by me and yet not mine. I am prepared to try, I think, but . . . but need some persuading. I can't help but wonder if we couldn't go down to a more universal level of those myth types – Miss Virgin and Ms Whore for example (if we end up splitting the voices you can be the virginal one). At the moment I'm infinitely more attracted to dragons and unicorns and so forth, actually: could one, culturally, do dragons for grown-ups without being cutesey?? If we're going to wave wands I think those fairytale creatures go very deep: a female Puss in Boots (avoiding too crude an interpretation!) might be interesting; but even more the great winged worms of folk tales – you know, griffins and phoenixes; could you enjoy a bestiary? If you are dead set on Eve/Mary we could combine these two desires and do a snake/dove polarity.

In the meantime, I have never read anything you have written that made me think 'trendy modernism' in the negative way we have been using it: I'd prefer to say an 'original and contemporary voice'. Also, try introducing the cynic to the muse – now there is a great idea for a

* *Daughter of Jerusalem*, Sara Maitland (Blond & Briggs, 1978)

book – *The Letters of the Cynic and the Muse* – we could do it in blank verse.

Take good care of yourself, this is a silly letter, but I wanted to show you my humour restored and my total confidence in this project. Keep chucking the ideas in. Oh, and I meant to ask you about witches?

Lots of love, Sara

Dear Sara,

Magic dragon and magic weevil. It's sounding good.

We could mix sexual politics with zoomorphic metaphor. I must say I like this trend much better than the myth stuff. I really don't want to write Eve in this context, though I would love to see what you do with Mary. Perhaps we can have Mary and not Eve? If we're assigning characters to one another, I think we should swap at half time, so that each of us shares the responsibility all down the line. And then neither of us can feel really proprietorial about characters. What do you think?

No, no, I am NOT suggesting we do a big nineteenth-century realist novel together – I was just voicing my incredible envy at the vast expanses of matter which those novelists dealt with and wishing I could give things the same attention. Conciseness, shorthand is now what we all write, with the visual mass media having made it unnecessary for writers to draw pictures with words. Anyway, I'm no good at that, really. I've never enjoyed writing landscape in prose and only sometimes in poetry.

Don't dismiss your comfort with classicism. You are rooted in it, your conversational language bears the same stamp as your written language. Your daring with subject matter works precisely because it can find sentence structures within which it is comfortable. So much for radical feminist rubbish about 'male' sentences being alien to female experience. Language is not *per se* male or female (as we both agree) and we must not confuse people's USE of language with language itself. The medium is, of course, the message but the message is not the medium. I think.

Yes, the bestiary gets me going. What about a whole lot of animals? If I can't have Mrs Noah, and I'm not letting her go completely, then what about the animals from the Ark? Or the Cynic and the Muse. Nice thought too. Are you saying you want to be the Muse? I suppose you should be; you do have the history and the geography, where I have neither.

Virgin and Whore; no way, unless I can be whore. Unless, of course, we do swap?

Witches? Forget it. They don't interest me at all. Dybbuks, lost and wandering souls, yes. That's a different thing. Witches are too frightening. I never met a good one. They're into power.

By the way, should we nudge Sam about this sodding contract? Every time I ring, the secretary mutters: 'in a meeting'. Last time, I even heard a loud 'Tell her (me) I'm in a meeting' – and it didn't ring true. Is the idiot going cold on us?

Love, Michelene

Dear Michelene,

That was a lovely letter. It had me jumping around juggling fluorescent balls: obviously there is something going here, along the bestiary/zoomorphic/Noah's Ark line (and a meeting of mythologies too). We could explore that: a homosexual dragon? Hackney Borough will be in ecstasies, but actually I am not uninterested in the concept – I have a deeply camp strain in my humour (the Anglo-Catholic legacy, or part of it) – which as feminist I have never found much use for in my writing which always makes me regretful.

I should say that I don't know much about Dybbuks – barring your *Guests in the Body*,* – or wandering souls, but I find the whole idea of possession infinitely more scary than that of witches, in fact too scary – so let's treat each other's fears with some courtesy, I think, and leave that chunk of material on the side (along with the nineteenth-century big realist novel; though I'd like to take up with you sometime the whole business of that large and brave canvas, which is the proper, true place of social realism and which has been totally abandoned for the petty realist novel – if I have to read one more novel about the adulteries of the intellectual upper-middle classes I shall go stark staring bonkers – though of course adultery like anything else can be a good image, for writing about something else).

What I do think is interesting is that you and I, however unrealistically, are almost entirely talking at the moment about *characters* rather than anything else – I mean, I suspect we are talking about voices, tones, narratives as well, but the formal question has been about which individuals we might use. Given our long

* *Guests in the Body*, Michelene Wandor (Virago, 1984)

discussions about the limitation of characterization I cannot help but find this interesting and wonder if it is one of the direct effects of writing a shared/collective fiction, and if so, does this need more exploring within the context of the book. I toss this off as a casual aside!

And thank you for your kindly remarks about classicism. Sometimes I want to be an entirely different sort of writer from what I am – hence my awe and veneration of poets – and sometimes I think there is zero you can do about how your links between imagination and language are formed; and yes, bold subject matter is easier in a language that is as cosy as an old dressing gown, or (better image) as well-fitting as a pair of new tights.

Mercifully we are at least in 100% solidarity about language *per se* and the use of language. However, what I would like to say about Sam at this point would be an abuse of language, however understood. I don't get it. Nicky wants the book, asks for the book, we agree to attempt the book. What more is needed to get a contract together??? If I thought it was about a struggle to get the best possible deal on the T-shirt rights, that would be one thing. But frankly I feel Sam just isn't very interested and probably wants both of us to write novels about the adulteries of the intellectual middle-classes. Rather than nudge, I'm more tempted to go straight to Nicky and say no contract by Christmas, no book. What do you think? I think they have something of their own going which we are insignificant to and either or both of them will sacrifice this one for whatever it is: however, we can hardly expect them to admit this. Damn, damn, damn.

Despite which, lots of love, Sara

My dear Nicky,

Just to let you know I have had a formal offer for Fraülein B which nudges into six figures. Can you match it? You know I would far rather you had it.

Best, Sam

My dear Sam,

Clever little you. Are you bluffing? Again? Yes, I can damn well match it. Can you be precise?

What's more, if you are not bluffing (and I will doubtless hear on the grapevine if you are), I will, as a special reward, find you an extra £500 for M and S if you can just get them to sign on the dotted line. To be honest I have a strong feeling that our list could use a little experimental flavouring – too many people seem to think we're getting too well packaged and I can even afford to drop something on the book in exchange for a little street cred.

Aren't we getting horrible in our old age? And if you ever tell them I said this I'll never buy another book off you again (except Fraülein B of course. How 'fictional' is it?? Can I meet her soon?).

With thanks and best wishes, also love, Nicky

Dear Winnie,

Weird is the understatement of the universe. She is totally potty.

All the joggling of the journey seems to have delayed winter-snooze time for us. But we're using the time, since we have to come back, to prepare our position carefully. Female-only lifeboats and special privileges for the hard-shelled are non-negotiable: positive discrimination is a soft option of course, since it suggests justice under the patriarchs is possible (shit: this underlining business is infectious; yeh we sneak glances at her gibberings). If you want to join us with a list of demands let us know: the tortifesto is pretty hot stuff, despite being prepared in the dark.

We're honestly looking forward to seeing you, and hope you manage to get through to us again soon.

In power, sisterhood and female-bonding,
Armorelle and Gertrude

Dear Mrs Noah,

Thank you *so* much for your letter. The owl delivered it *most* conscientiously, *what* a charming kind creature she is. Though I know the Bible calls owls unclean – though if that only applies to *eating* them, I *do* understand; I myself could *never* fancy one. Though there is that *wonderful* psalm about owls in deserts being teased and taunted, *you* know the one I mean. *But* I was brought up to think of them as wise and Athena's birds and things. *Anyway*, your letter did encourage me to keep going.

So I am on the road again, somewhere between Faversham and Canterbury, *I think*, and am writing this in the light of the moon and feeling like *a little girl* who has run away, which is an exciting feeling but also a *bit* scary.

I do not really *know* about Mr Vicar; when you talk about you and Mr Noah I think that you have what I understand is now called a *better relationship* than we do. I *suspect* that some of it is my fault because I have spoiled him dreadfully over the years, but you do not want to hear *about that*.

Do not worry about the pearls. When I did my degree at Oxford which was *ages* ago, of course, and I'm *afraid* rather a waste really, we did mediaeval literature and I remember *lovely* things about pearls: the pearl of *great price*, of course, and the oyster as the symbol of the soul, *opening* to the tides of God, taking in the gifts of the sea and using them to make something beautiful *inside*. On the nights when there is both a full moon and the evening star shining they leave their oyster beds and dance for the Queen of Heaven; and my mother gave them to me – my mother-in-law would *never* have done that. *How* sad for you to lose them, but *what* thrilling times you have lived through I could almost *envy you*, my life seems little and boring compared to yours, I hope you will not find me too dreary if we have to be on the boat together for a long time. But I will not sell them any more. They do feel *so lovely* on the skin, don't they?

By the way, on my journey I am working on a gift for *you*: I shouldn't tell you because it won't be a surprise but I have to because I am so proud of it and of me; it is the first time I have worked out a pattern so it is all my own. It was the Fair Isle socks that set me off; I am *knitting you a coat of many colours*, because I *never* cared for that show-offy youth, Joseph (not like Mary's Joseph, one of my favourites, *poor* boy, *not* the sort of life one would choose for one's children, really, is it? Sort of patient ox but *sweet*). Anyway, your *kind* owl friend brings in tufts and bits from her travels, and I sit in haystacks and barns by day and work on it.

I am keeping the tortoises *safe*, but I'm afraid they cannot find it in themselves to forgive me yet and we have had a few little *words*, I'm afraid – do you think they are what the newspapers call radical feminists? I am glad to hear you sounding so *happy* and I am definitely on my *way*.

Yours, Mrs Vicar

Armorelle and Gertrude,

Right, here it is. You are not the only ones who can reinvent the language.

I am a wormocrat. I know you'll think that's revisionist, but you're wrong. I believe in everyone having to prove their wormth to society. My principles are enwormed in Lenworm's dictum: 'Worm each according to worm needs, worm each according to worm abilities.' That's what I live by. If I was being given wormspitality in a comfy box, and being brought worm to people who love me, like you two are, I would be brimming over with the wormth of worman kindness, and not niggling and wormissiping all the time. Mrs Noah is keeping a corner of the hold worm for you; she has conceded that for hibernation your space will be a no-go area for males. But come the spring, you will have to accept the wormld as she is. Remember – the leaves you eat, the box you sleep in, were made by males. You cannot avoid men, though you are free to decide to worm you will relate. I am grateful to you for making me think about my language, but I wish you wouldn't force me into defending things that don't need defending.

Take care and sleep well.
Love, Winnie

PS I know you travel at night. Have you seen a bright light in the sky, ever, shaped like a unicorn?

Dear Mrs Vicar,

You're very clever, knowing all those things about owls and pearls. I just know things about people like what they like to eat and when they don't look well – as long as I'm not too busy with the resin.

I'm working on these glasses – spectacles – with which you can see a very long way away and even round corners. They can bend rays of light, as long as the eyes are right. I mean, they only work on some people – I'm not sure why, but when I put them on I can see right across to the middle of Poland, whereas poor old Noah can't see further than Paris. They're a by-product (from the waste, actually) of the expandable material the Ark is made of – it's marvellous to think nothing is wasted here. I suppose when you get here, we'll be a sort of commune thing ourselves, won't we?

And the coat of many colours! I can't wait. I've invented a substance to protect wool from sea spray, without it going all heavy and oily – so we can squirt it onto your twinsets. It would be a shame to spoil them. I suppose it will be exciting for the pearls to see the sea again – and you know all these poetic stories, that's so wonderful. I like the idea of pearls dancing for the Queen of Heaven; I suppose that must be what we see at night – and I can see now, with the moon full, and little white sparkles on top of the sea. I suppose it must be the reflection of all the pearls dancing on the seabed, not that I know whether there are pearls here, off Margate. I can hear an orchestra in the distance; probably Mr Edward Heath conducting in Broadstairs.

He was a very talented boy, you know. It was a pity he joined the Conservatives.

It must be very hard having to keep an eye on those silly tortoises. We're all rather annoyed with them for causing so much trouble. But don't tell them or they might run off again and then we'd never get away. About Mr Vicar, I just meant won't you miss him? I mean, really, I suppose if he doesn't want to come and you do, then you'll have to be apart for a while. But then you can always write, can't you? When we get too far from land for Tawny to deliver post, the albatross can take over. It's been terribly moody lately – restless to get back out to sea, I think, and it will give it something to do. We call it 'it' because we don't know whether it's male or female, and we've only got one anyway. They don't get on with ANYONE.

Please look after yourself and make sure you get enough sleep.

Mrs Noah

Dear Sr Mary Clare,

I have called round a couple of times and have not found you in. I would be grateful if I could make an appointment to come and see you, to discuss one Miss Frances Summers. She is wanted for questioning and we have information which leads us to believe you might know her whereabouts.

I would be grateful if you would ring the station to make an appointment. If I am not in, please leave a message.

Yours faithfully, Detective Inspector H Hound (CID)

Dear Detective Inspector Hound,

I prefer to write you this note after several attempts to speak to you on the phone, rather than leave a message. I think it would be better if I came down to the Station rather than you visiting here again, as – to be frank – some of the older Sisters have found your fellow officers rather disruptive. We are perfectly willing to assist the police in any way appropriate, but this is meant to be a convent and we value its peace, silence and serenity highly.

I have proposed to your office staff that I should visit tomorrow at 10.00 am when they seemed to think I would find you in. I hope this is agreeable, though it is fair to tell you in advance that I have never met Ms Summers and cannot imagine any way in which I can help you.

Yours sincerely, Sr Mary Clare, OSW

Dear Frankie,

Sorry I haven't written back before now; I had a septic cyst in my eye and then my babyminder quit (sometimes I feel that my most important relationships in the last ten years have been with my children's babyminders, which is a sad thought in one sense and a very healthy one in another).

I rejoice for you and your camel lady. I read once that the reason that camels have such haughty expressions is that, while human beings know ninety-nine of the names of God, camels know the hundredth. So ask her if she knows, or if she has even a clue. I am interested in the names of God myself. Are you?

If you left the diaries in England when you went, are they safe? It just this minute occurs to me that perhaps we are in the same family, because if you feel that the Dwarf belongs to you and I feel she belongs to me then perhaps she belongs to both and so we must be in the same family (although I have to admit that whenever I have read from that story, other people have recognized the kinship too).

I didn't realize before that you had been a feminist; because you said once in an earlier letter you didn't know much about feminism.

What community projects take place in a desert???

Take care of yourself and write if you can.

Yours, Sara

Winnie,

Look, we never meant to make you squirm. WE didn't even know you had a nose for us to get up. Perhaps we're a bit dim in the area of orifices; it is hard for us to imagine how it is for others because we have so many such complicated and beautiful ones; six external ones for legs, heads and tails, all retractable, plus the internal ones for eggs, food (in and out), breathing, etc. The infinite capacity of the tortoise for receiving and giving pleasure is one of the suppressed facts of life which is part and parcel of our oppression. So you like the dark, you live in the dark, perhaps being shut up in a shaky cardboard box (with no indoor toilet facilities we might as well add) is your idea of fun, but we are shell-shocked by it. So perhaps we didn't write as nicely as we should have last time; but you don't seem to understand, we're not selling a hard line, we're as home-loving as anyone (more so actually), but we think that people ought to be able to choose their own place and way to be. But thank you for the male-free hibernation space, that was pretty shelly of you, and will give us a home base from which to work.

The leaves we eat are not man-made; they grow naturally out of the sturdy patterned shell of Mother Earth. We are glad you are trying to think about language, but you can't have all the wormds (another slip; have you ever tried writing while skidding about in a box held by a lunatic vagrant, with pearls bonking about above your head every other minute?). We don't think you're revisionist, only that you have a faulty analysis, and given your oppression that is not surprising. Why don't you organize a revolutionary shell and do some consciousness raising until we are dragged in? Thank you for all your efforts, we know we need a larger group and are always prepared to negotiate on certain matters. I'm afraid we'll see you soon. Until then take care, stand firm, take things easy.

Yours, Armorelle and Gertrude

Armorelle and Gertrude,

If you find me a bit silent when you get here, don't worry. Frankly, I think that part of your trouble is that you're fighting off hibernation. After all, it is winter and you should be asleep. You MUST both relax or you will be entirely out of kilter with the seasons. Or is this part of your rebellion, refusing to respond to the earth and planets and the universe? If so, you're just in for misery. Really, the politics will wait till Spring. One doesn't have to be antediluvian to know that the wormld changes very slowly, even after wormvolutions. You see, I am trying to transfworm.

I look forward to seeing you – please relax.

Love from Winnie

Mrs Vicar,

How on earth have you managed to persuade them to give themselves up??? This morning, when I came out on deck to do my morning calisthenics, there they were, by the fire bucket. Two tortoises. I assume this is Armorelle and Gertrude? Since I have always operated on trust with those two sillies (which makes their rebellion all the more unnecessary) I never even bothered to take a shell-print in order to identify them. I say this with some trepidation – one tortoise can look to me very much like another. If it's A and G – then goody goody gumdrops. If it isn't, then we have some imposters on board, and we will have a boat meeting to decide what to do.

Mrs Noah

Dear Harriet,

I should have guessed. Well, there was no reason under heaven why I should have guessed, but I ought to have known we were bound to meet sometime and under the most complicated circumstances. When did you join the police? Why did you join the police? And even as I want to ask the questions I can hear yours: 'When did you become a religious? Why did you become a religious?'

A ghastly childishness overwhelms me – I want to say my uniform is prettier than your uniform. But you coped with the surprise better than I did. Did you know already?

At a more serious level, I think you will have to tell me more about why you want to speak to Frances Summers before I can decide whether I ought to tell you. And never threaten me again like that, please: bear in mind that many members, grandees even, of both my Church and the Church of England would love a nice legal battle about whether religious confidences are privileged in Court as they are in France.

I don't know whether to laugh or cry.

I will doubtless be hearing from you again, until when I think 'best wishes' is appropriate, don't you?

Sr Mary Clare

My dear Anita,

No, of course I didn't know. How could I? How could I possibly know that a nun whom I had to contact in the course of my duties would turn out to be Anita Sullivan, earnest, long-haired feminist from *Women's News*? We have both come a long way, haven't we?

I joined the police because I always fancied a nice uniform. Quite literally. Remember Tom? He was in the CID, though I didn't know it until we got back from holiday. The holiday romance that lasted. I was pretty shocked, but spending weekends in his Oxfordshire village made me feel that all our jargon attacking the pigs was just not realistic. The rest is history, really, and I can go into it at greater length if you like. But I drifted away from the group after that (you had already left, remember) since I didn't want to have to justify myself. And yes, I like the uniform, though I'd be happier if we could wear trousers. I am still campaigning, you see!

Anyway, we need to contact Ms Summers about some of her friends. I assure you that it isn't serious and will not necessarily involve her in any direct conflict with the police. We need some information from her, so if you would let me have an address, I would be most grateful. Interpol are trying but haven't got very far. Do let me know – and you must come round and meet Tom again. He is most amused at it all.

Best, Harriet

Dear Harriet,

Thanks for your letter. It was sort of a relief knowing about Tom because I was always upset by everyone's paranoia, even then, and certainly have been since, and it is nice to know that the people you gave such commitment to were not really totally crazed. Apart from the big fight with you it was the internal suspicion and self-aggrandisement that made me feel I had to leave. But sad. And complicated. And I should tell you that nun or no nun I still believe that the way the police function here, as in other countries, is unjust and therefore unholy, I mean structurally, not individually. Calling trousers-for-policewomen feminism seems a bit like calling a woman prime minister a great step forward for women's rights. But then, most people think the same about being a religious, so where are you?

Not sure about coming round and meeting Tom to be honest, there are old scabs best not picked – although that whole catastrophe is a large part of why I ended up in a nice uniform too, so I ought, if I were really saintly, to be grateful to the pair of you.

Thanks for coming through with the information about Frances Summers. Your office will have told you that I rang them with the address, as up-to-date as I have it.

Harriet, there is no more innocence among us any more. I am more upset than I should be at seeing you again. Somehow that fight, that group, that hectic time was crucial for me, but also I cut off from something, as obviously you have done too, and will never know whether that was for good or bad. Not sure I want to.

Anyway, this is all most inappropriate, I shall go to

Chapel; with a certain glee I shall sign off by saying that I will pray for you.

Sr Mary Clare

Dear Anita,

Well, I don't know. Nothing gets forgotten, does it, let alone forgiven? I suppose I was tactless, chirping on about you coming to have dinner with me and Tom. It must have looked as if I was flaunting him at you or something.

What we cut off from was each other. That's brutal and it's true. We were both scared.

What I suggest is that we don't talk about it. Not for a while. No more evasion. I'd like to get to know you all over again. And the first thing we could do is have a boozy dinner, just us two, so we can catch up on what we've both been doing for ten years. Then, if we still like each other, we could venture a little further and maybe you won't feel so bad about seeing Tom again. Oh dear. I'm sure nuns aren't allowed to have boozy dinners.

I'm at a loss. How is it proper for us to meet? After all, I take my uniform off when I finish work, but I imagine that you only take your uniform off when you go to bed. Oh dear. There I am again. Before I know where I am, I shall be having erotic fantasies about a nun.

I have got through a bottle of wine this evening, nerving myself up to write to you. I shall stick it in an envelope before I sober up. (The letter, not the wine!)

Harriet

Beloved Winnie,

How I have yearned for you since your star-sped letter came. I feel we are as one in the meeting place of polarities – you earth-bound, united forever to the heavy element, and I heaven-bound, united forever to the light element of air and dream.

I have cast thoughts and smiles upon you in my free roaming ever since, but alas – in as much as it is possible to disturb the glory of my wild racing – I have been disturbed and thus unable to pour the cool fires of my love upon you in its purity. A foolish woman has written a book* about me which distorts my internal verity and misrepresents me to the time-bound sphere. Her book is a curious mish-mash of madness and pain, I could feel for her in her mind-prison, but she has contaminated me – listen: 'The Unicorn is unique and it is male'; listen yet again: 'she would like, she thinks, to stay out late tonight and play with the white unicorn who comes to her dancing down the trail of the bright stars, seeking with love the milk from the breast of this pure virgin . . . to ride the sides of the steep mountain and sing until dawn.' Or, worst of all: 'The Holy Virgin Mary herself was seated on a throne of gold and jewels and the unicorn was at her feet'. That my tender and everlastingly precious relationship with that sweet but foolish Jewish girl should be so sullied, contaminated. It happens all the time, I try and struggle to float above it, to forgive and to rest on my own perfect dignity; it took me years, nay centuries as mortals call them, to recover from those appalling tapestries, and now this. Winnie, I feel sure that you will understand, because in your own small way you are so engaged with those over-domesti-

* *Virgin Territory,* by Sara Maitland (Michael Joseph, 1984)

cated reptiles, but it breaks my heart and touches my purity when humans steal from us our very beings and slot them into their foolish, bodily, idiotic stories. What can this woman novelist know of the glory of my soul, the pure being of bodilessness, the oneness with my own Idea. Sometimes I feel that the only human who came near to understanding was dear Carl Jung. It is unendurable and has to be endured.

But fear not, tiny friend, I will and do still float in the sparkling dark, and rejoice to see your safe and sturdy boat dance on the swelling bosom of the great and timeless, tideful ocean. Although I have determined that I cannot join this cruise, my love goes with you as you float, rocked in the arms of the sweet mother of all the living. What the foolish ones call ozone is the softness of my every exhalation, so fear not. Dear worm, remember, each dark moment of your deep movement brings the power of air and fertility to the depths of the loam of the Earth herself; and your own solitary purity of self-generation joins you with the great virgins of the dream world; it is the same as that of the great blue stars, and even of my own self.

I smile upon you, little one, and you will see my shadow in the turning of the moon.

Tenderly, Eustacia-Rose

Eustacia, my love,

My earth greets your air. But please – it is not heavy – I too am air, I create air, I am the beautiful contradiction which floats through the earth, which man (that's what they are called, though I have some friends who would get very angry and say that excluded women and tortoises . . . forgive me for bringing ugly reality into this) needs for food and support. Without me the earth would be heavy indeed, would so weight itself down that it would fall out of balance with the universe and hurtle swirling into the other dark universes, where there is no life and no love.

Please – don't worry about books and what is said about you. When people fear you, they will misrepresent you. I am seen as a coward in ordinary language, as surreptitious, secretive, rotten, something to destroy other people's pleasure. But I am the opposite, and although I can be hurt, in the end I know that I must rely on the time and place I inhabit, on where I come from. But anyway, the things you quote from this woman writer are very beautiful. The unicorn's love for the Virgin seems safe and good and true. This woman wants your serenity, wants to know what it is like to be at one with the air, to be so aware of yourself that you are entirely unaware, to not know where your body ends and your self begins, and vice versa. If putting things into words is her way of doing it, you should not fear. She cannot touch you as you are. And you and I know that we are safe. There is a saying that goes, 'Sticks and stones can break my bones, but words will never harm me' – I think we can borrow that from the mortals. Tapestries fade, but you never will. I never think of the Virgin as Jewish. I think they mentioned the Virgin once, when they were talking about – oh yes, they were playing a game that meant everyone had to say what they would like to have done if they could have had their lives over again. Mrs Noah (who is very sweet) said that if she had known that Mary and Joseph hadn't had anywhere to stay for the night, that the inn had turned them away, she'd have gone out and brought them round to her place. I suppose if she'd done that then what is called 'history' would have taken a very different turn. I mean, if the three kings had turned up with presents, Mrs Noah would have put them through the most terrible interrogation before she'd let them go anywhere near the baby. She's terribly fierce about her territory. I mean, that she will not let anyone she thinks might be an enemy near, but once she's accepted you she's loyal and will defend you for ever. She's actually prepared a marvellous hibernation space for the two tortoises, Armorelle and Gertrude, when they come back – they've run off with some crazy ideas – oh, I can't even begin to talk about it, it makes me so tired, but I think they're suffering from millenial angst. You know, fear of the flood, and reliving the separation anxieties from the time when they first came out of the sea – oh, you know, that stuff that evolutionists say. I haven't told Mrs Noah all this because she believes in the Seven Days story. But you and I know that We are One with the Universe. WOU. That is our belief, and even when I can't see you, when the moon has a hazy collar round her, when Sirius is faint, we both are assured in our own immaculacy.

Take care – until I aerate again in your direction.

All my love, Winnie

Winnie,

Do something! Of course they're not bloody well us. They are certainly some foul bourgeois heterosexist imposters trying to muscle in on our place on the Ark; and before you try and wriggle out of it by saying we never wanted it anyway, we want to say that that is absolutely not the curve. We, Armorelle and Gertrude, were given the right to decide the future of tortoise species identity: how often do any females, let alone gay ones, silenced as we are by history and culture, get a chance like this? Now we'll see the limits of Mrs Noah's much-vaunted liberalism; we bet you that when she finds out she'll take them in preference to us: heterosexual privilege as *always*. We're writing to you because you've always been our friend and in any case we're not talking to her. 'One tortoise can look to me very like another' – a humanist pig. When humans talk like that about each other it's called racism, but come to the more important species and they can't be bloody bothered to learn.

You'll probably bury your head (and the rest of you) in the ground and ignore our rights, but please Winnie, stand up for yourself and us. A boat meeting – by Tort, that's outrageous (if nothing else we have a very close relationship with certain aspects of the LAW)!

From our angle, this whole thing is getting crazier by the moment. Mrs V is in a bit of a decline, missing her bourgeois privileges, we suspect; here she is with a chance to explore the real tortuous issues of radical feminism and all she can do is sit about wringing her pearls and sniffling. We're having to look after her, read her letters to her and make sure she puts on her twinsets when it's cold (only because we now realize she's the only chance we've got to get to the Ark and dig in for our rights). It makes the Patty Hearst case look simple: she only came to agree with her tortnappers, we have to bloody well look after ours. And we're lost again. Couldn't you ask Mrs N to send someone useful – a horse, an elephant or a camel or someone – to pick us up? I suppose that would be against her principles of freedom for all. Liberal garbage; we demand positive discrimination for everyone with legs under two and a half inches long. And we're not coming at all until those scabs are out. The crawling toads – a disgrace to tortoise solidarity, they should have their shells stripped from their backs. And how did they get out to the boat anyway. A lot of heads are going to roll when we catch up with them; the shells of tortoises grind slow but they grind exceeding small – so watch out.

Armorelle and Gertrude

Dear Michelene,

I'm afraid I've been away again, hence no immediate answer to your letter. I went to York for General Chapter – the meeting of all the sisters in my Order; it was meant to be only a day, but Mother dropped a bomb by announcing that she wanted to retire (she's quite allowed to, but in our house it has never happened before). So we had three days of heavy politics, discussions, vetting each other – in a spread-out Order like mine you really don't know everyone well enough: all very C P Snow.

With all the will in the world I simply don't understand what you're saying about Jewish nationhood, Jewish culture and Jewish religion; because the analogy you give doesn't work quite – when you say, like being brought up in a Christian State stamping you with its values. Leaving aside the fact that I question whether this (or anywhere else) is a 'Christian State' in the way that Israel is a Jewish State, you too were brought up in this country. I know it is not the same, but I suppose I think (possibly because of being an Old Testament person primarily) that Jewishness is something more or other than over-against-ness???

Extraordinary how hard it is to write about, with that I quite agree. Seized at every turn with fears of liberal guilt and not sure what is 'prickly' and what isn't; and also – to my own surprise – a *misplaced* desire to defend Catholic Christendom against the charge of anti-semitism. Since this clearly is *not true*, I find my own reaction revealing – though of what I couldn't say.

At least with the woman/feminist/socialist we have some common ground, I think.

Yours affectionately, Sr Mary Clare

Dear Sr Mary Clare,

I hope my cream-tea effort to explain how I see the distinctions between Jewish religion, nationalism and 'culture' made some sort of sense. I think, though, that we both forgot the question you raised in your letter – when you said that you didn't think England was a 'Christian' State in the way that Israel was a 'Jewish' State. Perhaps our difference here is that (correct me if I'm wrong) you don't believe that we live here in a Christian State because it isn't Christian enough for you? I was trying to describe the objective religious allegiance given by a State to the Church; for example, public holidays fall according to the Christian calendar; Sunday is the more official day of rest (viz all the rows about Sunday opening times in shops). In the same way, of course, Israel observes the structural dictates of the Jewish religion; but I think in both countries there is not necessarily a total follow-through – ie, here only about 2% of the population go to church (the same percentage go to the theatre, apparently – the statisticians don't say whether it's the same 2%) and not all Israelis are strictly kosher, etc.

Anyway, this is merely a sort of thank-you letter. I must say I had the most curious feeling, as if I knew you very well and could feel quite free to say anything – if not now, then some other time.

I look forward to seeing you again.

Yours, Michelene

Dear Sara,

You are a true friend. I'm really sorry about your eye – yes, I did know you have children, because various of our mutual friends have told me about them. Oh yes, I felt great after sorting Grace out. Mind you, she keeps turning up in my damn dreams, as if she was real, and still alive – but then she isn't, so I just shake my head, have a good strong cup of coffee and get on with things. I have read all the stories and novels you've written, and I wrote to you in the first place because I felt that you would understand me because you understood my great-great-great- (I think that's right) grandmother so well. I feel so honoured that you could share your thoughts about writing with me – I think this is what true sisterhood is about, don't you? Perhaps it's no coincidence that it's called sisterhood anyway, our way of making our own families. Michelene has a poem about Virginia Woolf* in which she says something about that. Have you read it?

My camel lady is something else. She is working on a community play here and I will ask her if the camels have told her the hundredth name of God. But I think she's Jewish, so she may well not wish to know that. We have talked about everything under the sun except religion.

I still think you're wrong to be romantic about the desert. I hate it. I'm only here because my red-haired love (she's called Ruby) has a stubborn commitment to live out here for a while.

Love from Frankie

* *Gardens of Eden*, op. cit.

Dear Frances,

Suddenly it seems better to call you that. This morning I met with a police officer who wanted to know a lot of things about you although she would not say why. Most of them I could not tell her because I did not know, but she was very pressing that I should tell her your address, and it seems proper that I should tell you as soon as possible that I did so. I do not know what is best to do. It is very difficult for me as it turns out that this policewoman is someone I once knew very well, and who knows a great deal about me. Perhaps I am making a drama out of nothing and she only wants to return your lost passport or something of that nature, however she is rather a highly placed police officer and I doubt it. Now I feel confused and guilty towards you and involved in your situation in a way that neither of us ever intended. If I can do anything to help, please let me know. Please answer this letter promptly.

Yours, Sr Mary Clare

Dear sodding sister and I don't think,

You fucking cunt, turning me over to the fuzz. You can certainly do something for me. You can get the fuck out of my life and forget you ever sent me your measly patronizing charity.

Frankie

Dear Frankie,

Am I allowed to say that I am sorry. The police assured me that you were not wanted for anything serious; if the officer concerned lied to me then I have been a complete fool.

You may not want to get this letter and you don't have to answer it, but if there is anything I can do to help please do ask – now or at any time in the future.

Yours, Sr Mary Clare

Sara,

You shit. I am leaving Alice. Don't expect to hear from me again.

Frankie

Dear Frankie,

What the hell am I supposed to have done?

I can think of nothing in my last letter that was that offensive.

What is going on?

Are you OK?

At least tell me what has happened.

Sara

Dear Michelene,

Thank you for your note; yes, I too enjoyed myself enormously. This may sound odd but it is extraordinarily nice for me to talk to someone who isn't a Christian and doesn't care whether I care. Although I do meet quite a number of non-Christians, they tend, on spotting my habit, to be either apologetic or aggressive about it. I'm sorry I haven't written before, too, but what with winding up the term and then getting organized for Christmas it has been a little hard. As you can see from the address I'm now out of London and in fact have gone 'home' for Christmas – that is to the Mother House (anything you may read that suggests nuns abandon family life is a misrepresentation: we simply replace the infant model with a larger, more demanding one); and of course this Christmas is alarming because everyone, including I should say me, is politicking like mad about our new Mother Superior; the election will be at Epiphany. There is practically no one else I could say this to so you'll have to grin and bear it: nuns politicking is pretty disgusting because everyone pretends that the Holy Spirit will whizz in and settle the matter, but in fact all of us are willing and eager to assist the Holy Spirit and electioneer away while pretending that we aren't. By and large the recognition that the Holy Spirit works not by lightning bolt but by the works of human beings is accepted in theory but not in practice so everyone has to pretend, pretend, pretend all the time. It is weary-making, difficult and terribly, terribly important: we are electing a someone we're supposed to be in obedience to, you see. Well. . . .

Much nicer to think about tea and some of the very interesting things that have come up in my mind since then. One point which I think has got lost that I really did want to ask you about, is the fact that you too, although Jewish, were brought up in a 'Christian country' and I wonder what effect this had. I was fascinated to hear about the years you spent in Israel, and still wonder if you would have another go at explaining why it didn't work out for your family. The point you raise in your letter about whether my problem is about England 'not being Christian enough' is quite interesting to me, having been a child in Ireland – which is much more overtly a Catholic Country – and having trained in Rome, as I said, which is of course Catholic in the fullest and most nourishing sense except that Italians don't think so. I knew, when I realized that I was headed for the nunnery, that I definitely wanted not to work in Ireland and chose one of the very few international teaching Orders which doesn't have an Irish house. And that was definitely *not* from any evangelical, converting zeal. Of course, Ireland is not the easiest place for a rather intelligent, middle-class Roman Catholic girl to be; but I really did want to be somewhere where Church and State were not so interlinked. It remains, however, strange to hear (whether accusingly or pridefully) people calling GB a Christian State; this may of course be a reaction against the way that term is used by the present government, but not entirely. It's not that the Church has always been perfect indeed, but the implication that the desperate inequalities are somehow our fault is hard to deal with – especially as philosophically they may well be our fault in some deeper way. When I first started trying to read feminist things I was always deeply hurt by the passionate rejection of what was always called the Judeo-Christian tradition, which seemed to be blamed for everything which I had been taught was precisely the fault of the Hellenic tradition of dualism in which the Church found itself. Now, of course, biblical scholarship has shown that 'the Church' did not spring to life in quite that fully fledged way we imagined . . . I'm rambling, but it does seem worth considering that the State of Israel itself is still engaged in continuing historical development just as the Church's relationship with politics and culture is in this country.

Looking back over what I have written, I'm not sure how much sense it will make to you – if any. Like you, I sensed some really quite profound correspondences between us in our conversation, relaxing and lovely, but I must not let that delude me that we share the same chunks of knowledge. Nor even indeed the same perspectives. I do realize that what feminism, for example, is to you is quite different from what it is to me; and obviously that goes for religion too.

I'm not sure if it's appropriate to wish you a Happy Christmas; would you prefer to be wished a happy time during Christmastide? I do wish it anyway.

And someone has sent me Sara Maitland's last novel for a Christmas present. Have you read it? Will I like it?

Yours, Sr Mary Clare

Dear Sara,

Fluorescent balls, eh. Well, well. Hi-tech pornography, is it? At least if we do that then we carefully avoid the boring intellectual middle-class adultery bit. The problem is that it isn't all boring really; it's just that you have to believe wholeheartedly in all the pros and cons of marriage to make it work. You also have to believe in romantic love, etc, etc, and if I could really get going on that, then I'd do a Mills and Boon. Which seems to be another of the trendy things at the moment. All these right-on feminists (whisper, whisper) secretly writing Mills and Boon under jolly floral pseudonyms. Why, you might be one. And indeed, methinks the lady doth protest too much and I might be one. In the cynical climate of the 1980s I think, if only I could. Perhaps that is what Nicky really wants. Perhaps the caveats against flogging our feminism too fiercely in Nicky's first letter were a subtle hint. Aha. If that is the case then we really want a REAL advance, eh.

No, I don't think we're talking about characters. Voice, yes. That is what it is. The characters don't exist until we've written them. We're also only talking about which individuals we might use as points of departure. Once we've decided and got going, we will create our own, with whatever baggage of personal knowledges and needs and associations we want to lay on them and on each other.

I think re Nicky and Sam that something funny is going on. Let's give them until Christmas, during which time you and I can go on discussing things, and if we have something sorted between us by then, we can go to them with a simple 'do you want it or not?' If we get no decent offer within a week of doing that, let's offer the book to someone else. We've got enough contacts between us to get that going. This being on the assumption that Sam doesn't want to handle it – and at the moment I see no signs that that is the case. You and I both know that when an agent wants to get an offer from a publisher they can do it in a week easy; even with today's marketing boffins heading the delicate business of book publishing. Incidentally, if we get this contract sorted, we must also get an early commitment to a decent publication month. My most recent publisher's horror story was on my most recent non-fiction tome; bust a gut to deliver last May, to give them time to bring it out next Jan/Feb; great enthusiasm, send it to the copy editor, I get the copy-edited copy to check, I send it back with a fair number of changes, saying I hope this doesn't need to be retyped, I hope the book is still on schedule; the buggers keep it on their desks for months, and now turn round and offer me a July publication ('offer' being a polite word for 'inform'). I freak, since July and August are bum months for books . . . drift, drift, drift and the editor had the gall to try and blame me for the delay. Sorry for letting off steam. I'd like to avoid that happening with this. Mind you, I say that every time.

Love, Michelene

Dear Michelene,

Obviously we should do some soft-core, hi-tech pornographic romance about Mrs Noah's relationship with a boll weevil.

The rather more pressing question if you ask me is whether we should do it at all. This is not doubts about the viability of the creative project, but about its professional viability. I think Nicky and Sam are behaving like minor characters in one of those enormous Victorian realist novels we talked about earlier – they're running a sub-plot of their own which is bound to affect the heroines of the piece (you and me), but we don't yet know what it is (in a real novel of this sort one or both of them would turn out to be one or both of our long-lost parents and/or children, but I have not the patience to read on until I find out which). I hate the way my energy is drained and my enthusiasm cramped by this sort of carry-on – I hate it in myself because I ought to be tougher and I hate it in them because I ought not to have to be tougher. So 100% yes, I take your point about giving them till Christmas although that's generous of us; it is going to be hard to offer around though, despite our contacts, until we have some text – what seemed good about this is that it came from Nicky and apparently gave us free rein.

Your tale of gloom does not depress me as much as it ought to (brief pause to say, 'poor you, what a bugger') because it is absolutely typical. And I don't know how to avoid it: writers should of course be better 'organized' but God knows how – the plight of all piece-workers is a traditionally crummy one and when it's messed up with concepts of the Artist, and the loose egos including mine that are waving themselves about . . . drift, drift, drift as you so rightly say. Of course, I'd like to avoid all that with this one, and of course, as you also point out, I say that every time.

So, Nicky must come up with an answer by Christmas. Sam must be persuaded to build in some sort of consultation about cover/publication date/etc, or we might as well agent ourselves. Then all we have to do is write the damn thing, which feels easy compared to this lot. Do you want to get together and co-write a letter?

Anyway, it would be nice to see you.

Love, Sara

Dear Sara,

As and when we get down to it, yes, we seem to have a lot of ideas to play around with. Though I notice you have gone rather quiet about Mary recently. However, I shall bring her up again and try to persuade you.

On the other matter: frankly, I don't give a shit what the Nicky-Sam sub-plot is. Both are being very unprofessional, but that does seem to me par for the publishing course. When I began, long-haired, fringed, mini-skirted, and a little (not much) less cynical than now, when I began earning money, doing freelance bits and pieces for publishers, editorial skill was highly prized, spelling and punctuation seen as important and I had to watch my Ps and Qs. At the same time, there was the odd editor who would let you go loopy with experimenting with type faces, spelling, punctuation, etc.

Now we seem to have sodding mediocrity: neither the old-fashioned Shorter Oxford Dictionary skills nor the American-style careful textual editorship, and not even the nutty freak who wants to make with the experimental. Of course, I generalize like crazy, and occasionally I come across someone who swears by their editor. Having never worked with Nicky before I don't know into what category that relationship will fall (perhaps it will be the exception that proves the rule, and we all seek for the one true romantic love, however often we've been let down, don't we?) – but, I must cease the lecture on the ideology of the relations of literary production and return to the point.

Yes, let's compose a letter to Sam. Meanwhile, let's decide just between the two of us to start on the book anyway. It will be fun to get going – and if we are yet again falling into the ineluctable trap of starting work before we have seen sight of a contract, then so be it. While on principle I normally don't set type to paper until I've signed on the dotted line, this is a bit different, and I don't want the horrors of publishers censoring our imaginations. They have too much influence on us as it is.

Love, Michelene

Dear Sr Mary Clare,

You are such a challenge and source of envy to me, since whatever your heresies, you have an institutional context for your beliefs and my little system of ethics which I struggle to keep alive has absolutely nothing external that I can identify as an institution. I envy you your alternative 'family' life. I spent a little while on a kibbutz many years ago, and hated every single bloody second there, but it still stands in my mind as the sort of model which ought to work, which has all the preconditions for support and context. But of course once you have that you also have the possibility of transgression, exclusion and exile. So you can't win. I must be a terrible old moralist at heart.

I hope you had a good Christmas. I had a boring one, which suits me fine, as I always get ill and depressed and can't wait till it's all over and New Year's Eve is gone and I can put a different date on my letters.

I can't really entirely explain about being Jewish and brought up in a Christian country, except that feeling alien is an everyday condition. Every morning at school reminded me that I did not belong – Assembly. And at the same time I was not religious, so I didn't belong in the room where I waited with the 'other' religion' kids. I can see that from your point of view there is a separation between Church and State, but that is a very fine point of distinction within a broad church, as it were; I do not even take up one of the options within that Church. And of course I don't belong to any other 'church', so I can't even be content in a comparative way. Being Jewish is being very comfortably underground – I mean, you can be an atheist (a good Marxist feminist like I have become – well, good is perhaps questionable) and still feel passionately Jewish. It's there in the language (Yiddish) in – oh dear, what am I about to say – a funny sense of family and recognition is there. I have always felt far more affectionate about/towards American Jews than English Jews, because the dominant American culture is itself so imbued with, formed alongside, the immigrant sensibilities of Jews. England, of course, has its own immigrant population, but unlike the US, where all white populations are essentially immigrant populations, England has its good old solid white, indigenous population, who have a wonderful class confidence which cuts like a knife. The crude effect that growing up in England had on me is to make me a sort of permanent exile who can't live anywhere else. But then that has been the condition of Jews throughout history, so in that sense I ought to feel secure and part of history. I am of course also very English and my entire literary education has been in the English language. But I have many other languages as well, and it is those I have been exploring recently and *Gardens of Eden* is an example of that – which I think was where we came in.

I found what you said about Catholicism and Ireland very interesting. It makes sense, I must say. I was not describing GB as a 'Christian State' in order to put it down; just that the official and dominant religion in this country is Christian and that is a fact. I didn't mean that everyone who called themselves a Christian would necessarily like the form of that fact, but that whereas you engage with it (even by opposition, perhaps) I do not. If, for example, I lived in Israel, which I wouldn't, the way things are, I would perhaps have a parallel relationship to that State as you have to the British one. Engaging from within.

Does that clarify anything?

Yes, I have read Sara's novel and think it is tough, characteristically full of solid substance and very, very interesting. I have no idea whether you will like it – whether you will be shocked by the way she writes the nun – though I suspect you will approve of the ending. Sara is a marvellous and scholarly stylist who dives into dangerous waters and chooses disturbing content. She is also – as a writer – rather amoral, I think (in her choices not her message, which is very moral), and pretty well always gets away with it, I think. In fact, I think it is the tension between her knowledge of (dare I say it) hell and the security of her cultural heritage that provides the tensions and excitements of her writing. If you've read any of the reviews (of course – you say you have) don't take any notice – or not too much. Most of the straight reviewers are terrified of reading about the people she writes about, and so curtain themselves from her skill and demandingness. The trendy ones always want it easy so ignore those too. But I suppose it depends on whether you feel at all protective about the experiences of nuns appropriated for fiction.

Do let me know what you think about it.

Yours, Michelene

Nicky,

The offer for Fraülein B is £100,000, but I have had another nibble at £125,000. I'd like to get it tidied up quickly, so if you can persuade yours to top it – the hottest property of the decade, I promise you . . .

Thanks for the upped offer for M & S. I've passed it on, but I don't think the writers' collective is going to bite. It has to be divided two ways, goes their argument. I really think they overestimate this one. Perhaps you are marginally to blame for such initial enthusiasm; not of course that I would ever object to publishers encouraging writers, but possibly your goodwill outran your normally impeccable professional judgement. You may be able to tell that I am a little weary of this. If you are sure that this is your final offer *vis-à-vis* M & S, I will tell them. If they're unhappy with it, we can get back to the real book business. I hear on the grapevine that there will be a sequel to Fraülein B, in the person of Prince Casimir's diaries, would you believe.

Interested? Over a bottle of Beaujolais Nouveau?

Ever, Sam

Dear Mrs Noah,

Oh dear; everything seems terribly difficult doesn't it. The tortoises who were just beginning to calm down, even snuggle in, for their winter nap (I had given them some of my wool scraps to make them more comfy) are all stirred up again, and snappish and mean. And it isn't my fault that it is hard to find fresh lettuce in what everybody should know is hop- and apple-growing country, but since you warned me against tortoise-shell combs I don't think it was very tactful to say you couldn't tell one tortoise from another. And what with the lettuce problem and the Mr Vicar problem and the getting trapped in Canterbury by that dreadful Canon who trained with Mr Vicar and having to stay two whole nights with him so that he shouldn't suspect I was running away; I told him I was looking for an antique desk as a Christmas present for Mr Vicar, so that he wouldn't tell, and that all my usual clothes had been stolen on the train, which though I say it myself I thought was rather clever of me, don't you; but then his wife assumed that the tortoises were a present for her really rather disagreeable little son and she insisted on taking me round about fifty antique shops and putting the tortoises in the garage which did not help their tempers I'm afraid and then when we did get away we got dreadfully lost because I got all muddled up between Margate and Dover (silly billy, aren't I) and then I'm sorry to say I got into a bit of a state with it all and the tortoises really did try to be kinder, but honestly they are not terribly sensitive when you come right down to it and anyway that is why I haven't written for a bit and I am extremely sorry, really and truly.

Anyway I once read somewhere that you always got a really first-class Christmas dinner in prison, and at least it will be the first one that I haven't *had* to cook for *goodness* knows how many years, so I got myself arrested for vagrancy, *of course* giving a false name, well at least I *meant* to get arrested for *vagrancy* but being me of course I messed it *up* and have actually got arrested for *soliciting* which *is* rather embarrassing and I don't *quite* know what Mr Vicar will say when he hears about it because he really does *want* to be made Area Dean and I don't think I've ever *heard* of an Area Dean whose wife had – I *think* it is called – *done time*. So I'm having a peaceful little *rest* and they will send me on my way after Christmas so unless something *else* goes wrong, which would not surprise me, I think I should be with you at about New Year and I am really looking *forward* to it. I hope after all this *trouble* you will still want me, but at least the *knitting* is making good progress and I've been allowed to keep the tortoises *with* me, although that did require a little prevarication which, of course, *normally* I would not be able to approve of. *And* I am organizing the carol concert, which *is* something of a forte of mine and the choir is much *more* cooperative than the Sunday School, thank *goodness*.

I expect you don't *have* Christmas on the Ark which is an extra reason for prison because, *while* I would hate to inconvenience you *as you know*, when you have been so *kind* to me, I still think that I *might* miss the Midnight Mass, but now everything will be alright, except that our little postal system is tricky from here and you *may* not hear from me again until I am finished with these rather *unusual* Christmas festivities.

Your *silly* friend, Mrs Vicar

Dear Mrs Vicar,

Look – please just get here as soon as you can. I'm sorry you had to stay in prison over Christmas, but you probably had a better Christmas dinner there than you would have here because here we don't have Christmas dinner anyway, and I did a lentil stew and then got all caught up in my new invention which is a transparent set of wings which you can put on and fly over solid objects and you are held by gravity a pre-set distance from those objects, so you will never bash into anything or get hurt. But it doesn't yet work over water, so I'm working on that – anyway I forgot about the stew and it burned, and I screamed at the boys because they were all lying around watching *Some Like it Hot* and they didn't notice the smell of burning. Lazy shits, they are. And Noah's got a cold and can't smell much anyway.

Anyway, I'm still keeping a look-out for you and we gave the stew to the camels who now want it every day.

I don't know –

Your frazzled, Mrs Noah

My dear Mrs Noah,

Here we are! I'm afraid I borrowed a boat from the beach pool when we arrived finally, late last night; I do seem to be getting dreadfully immoral – the corrupting influence of my time among the criminal classes perhaps! (Just my little joke.) As it is three in the morning, I thought I wouldn't wake you up, but the tigers have been surprisingly friendly and I'm going to curl up with them and try to keep warm until the morning. I'm so excited! So I will just stick this little note on the kitchen table; what a nice kitchen you've got. I'll keep the tortoises with me I think as it is rather a large boat and I don't want them wandering off. I won't let them out of the box until I open it before your very eyes.

I am happy to be here and looking forward to meeting you at long last tomorrow, or rather today, isn't it.

Much love, Mrs Vicar

Dear Mrs Vicar,

I am writing this in felt-tipped pen so as not to wake you up. I know I was right to invite you – someone as resourceful as you, who can row a boat out to us – just what we need, in case, God forbid, we should have to go manual.

We must have missed each other by about an hour; I got up at four and found your lovely note. Anyway, it's now midday and you're still sleeping so I've covered you with my duvet, and in case you wake up and wonder where you are, this note will welcome you and give you some idea of what to expect. We are a bit chaotic as you'll see, but everything works well really.

Now. First of all, when you leave the tiger room, turn left and half-way along the corridor you'll find our living room. As with everything else, the walls are made of expandable resin so that we can make it larger or smaller as we need. There is obviously a space-continuum problem with this kind of thing since you can't expand all the rooms at the same time – so we have a rule whereby only one space is expandable at any given time and I control the mechanism. You'll soon get the hang of it. Nothing like seeing something in practice, I always say.

In the living room you'll find the automatic microwave which will have your breakfast in it. There will also be an electronic message which will light up when you go through the door – it's programmed to respond to you: I've shown it a sample of your handwriting and it can trace the three-dimensional form of Mrs Vicar herself from that information and it will know you when you walk in. It will switch on breakfast and by the time you're sitting at the table it will be cooked and ready. I've embroidered a serviette with your initials, actually

I just put Mrs V because I don't know your other name . . .

Enjoy your breakfast – and don't worry about the washing up.

Now, when you've eaten, go wherever you like and have a look round. All the animals know you're coming and by the time you wake up the tigers will have told everyone you're here. They are the biggest gossips out. I'll catch up with you sometime during the day – oh, ask anyone where my room is and help yourself to any clothes you need.

I must stop now because I am still working on the flight machines – look forward to seeing you later. We'll have dinner together at 7.00. I like early nights.

The tortoises are best left sleeping, I think. We shall probably have some trouble with them. Oh, Noah is pleased you're here, though a little shy at the thought of another woman on board. I thought he was past all that sort of thing. Silly boy.

Mrs Noah

Dear Harriet,

Thank you. You're braver than me; but I'm braver than I was then. Life is a bit hectic since I have recently been promoted and consequently have moved out of London (in all 'official' capacities you must now address me as Reverend Mother – I titter slightly myself).

But this, and other things this year, has made me realize I need non-church people so much in my life. Two months ago I'd have said, 'Forget it'; now I say, I have a meeting in London on the eighteenth and nineteenth. We could do a (moderately) boozy dinner in any (moderately) cheap restaurant near Westminster that you know of. No Tom. Not yet. I'm still praying.

Please let me know, MC

Dear Anita,

Terrific. The eighteenth is best for me.

Give me a ring when you get to London (work or home) and I'll tell you where I've booked.

This one's on me.

Harriet

Dear Michelene,

Thank you so much for your letter; it arrived at a time I dearly needed it. This letter will probably come out as a bit of a moan, I'd better warn you, because I don't know anyone else I can possibly moan to. I have been elected Mother Superior of our Order: I can't even pretend that it never crossed my mind because of course it did.

It's a very difficult thing to deal with, though. St Benedict in his *Rule* (the kind of model on which all the rules of religious life are more or less based) made 'scheming to be Abbess' number one on his list of grave faults – the punishment for which has always half-jokingly been held to be 'being successful in your schemes'. And, as I suggested in my last letter, we did sort of scheme, me and my lot, for political control of the direction of the Order. A bit late in the day I realized that, as the Third World weren't going to find an American Sister acceptable, and everyone wanted someone in their forties and someone with current teaching experience and someone who hadn't recently lived at the Mother House, and someone with reasonable academic standing, etc, etc, there were not too many possibilities.

You probably don't know why it is so scary though. There are now 1,864 women spread throughout the world who owe to me in person that obedience which is proper to Christ. Our whole training and way of life is supposed to be based on humility, obedience, self-denial, electing out of power games – and I end up about as powerful as any poor woman is likely to get in this world. I shall have to move up here which seems cold and isolated and reminds me of the very difficult years I spent in the novitiate (I wasn't one of those nuns who found it easy or natural). And there are piles and piles of administrative things I have to do. And already I find I miss London, particularly the collegiality that I enjoyed at the Seminary – both with the other staff people and with the students. And I chose to be a nun in part because I didn't want to be anybody's mother, and now I have this whole family of 'daughters'. I won't bore you with the spiritual stuff – unless you're interested – but I really need an outsider's ear to pour a great weight of self-doubt, wrong motives and fears into; poor you. I also need to think about something entirely other and will turn back to your letter.

I think that some of what you say about Jewishness applies equally to our 'oppositional' position (and I'm not clear how oppositional I really am). There is that inner conviction that Catholicism is the centre of Western Culture, even when the practice of the faith is of the shabbiest kind. All other Christians – in the depths of most RC hearts – are 'fringe'; they had to be Protestors because the middle ground was firmly occupied and we have the great artists (in school-terms) and the great City of Rome, so to speak, definitively tied up. So that, when I'm honest, Catholicism gives me a strange sort of confidence towards the non-Catholic world, while filling me with doubt and insecurity about being a 'good Catholic'. Does that make any sense at all? I would be interested in talking to you also about your time in the kibbutz because it has seemed, to several of us who want to think creatively about 'community', to offer a model of the 'alternative family' that we could usefully know more about. The religious orders have always been founded on the principle that sexuality and community life are antithetical – or rather that you had to choose, no one could have the lot, so to speak. Of course once you've chosen, the structure of the choice goes very deep; I can't say that I yearn after a more active sexuality; but I also can't say with any confidence that I wouldn't have yearned if I thought there was any possibility of getting both the community life and active sexuality. I know that the idea of 'sublimation' is extremely unfashionable; what's interesting is that for a lot of people it really does seem to work: those novelists who would have you believe that convents are packed full of seething repression of all sorts are simply wrong.

I'm half-way through Sara Maitland's novel, incidentally. My reading time has been, as you can imagine, rather disrupted. So far I have been reduced to shouting aloud at the author and the characters and at the religious Order (mine and hers). The voices of the Fathers seem horribly real to me although my voices are rather more benign – but would they be if I wasn't a thoroughly good nun; the sort who gets herself elected Superior of a fine progressive Order? Oh help!

Please, under no circumstances, address me as Mother. (Probably it would not have occurred to you to do so, which is why I can write to you. My own mother did, and with such pride and joy in her letter, it nearly broke my heart.) I don't suppose you might be interested in coming to my Installation: it's on the Feast of Candlemas – February 2nd – you might find it interesting in some ways and I would love to have you. But I know you don't like to travel much and shall understand if that seems a very alien thing. Please write again if you have time.

Yours, Mother Mary Clare

Dear Mary Clare,

(hope this is now appropriate, given that no, I don't feel I can address you as 'Mother')

I think that despite your doubts and whatevers, congratulations are in order from me. Or, if it were a Jewish Order which it ain't because there aren't any – now there's a job for a good liberal Jewish feminist – I would say Mazeltov, which is Hebrew for 'Good Luck': not a wish for it in the future, but a congratulation that fortune has smiled upon you.

Yes, you are caught in a marvellous dialectic, or when you're not feeling happy about it, contradiction. Does this mean – forgive my ignorance – that you have a hotline to the Pope? I am sure that despite your doubts you really wanted to become Mother Superior, and I am sure you will do a good job. It is ironic that just as my 'family' – two lovely, if sometimes infuriating sons – have now left – both to go to university (thank goodness they got in) – you have acquired your new charges, your 'daughters' as you describe them. I presume this means that you have no power over any men in the Church?

I do see exactly what you say about Catholicism being for you the centre of Western Culture. Of course, it would have to be. That makes total sense to me. It is precisely that sense of placing which I don't have at all. I don't even feel that Judaism is the 'true' religion, though I have to confess that I do believe I am the chosen people (obverse of CLASSIC WRITER'S PARANOIA?), and I do think Jewish people are more exciting and funnier and more tragic than anyone else. Oh, inverted racist that I am.

My time in a kibbutz will probably be of no use to you at all – I was nine when I went there and then I went back briefly to another kibbutz when I was twenty-one. Honestly, Israelis are really not always nice people (not anti-semitism, I assure you – quite the contrary) to someone brought up in the effete, arty West. They can be rough, tough, loud, emotionally brutal, macho (yes, the women too, even the feminine ones). Part of me glories in this because it is the obverse of the pale, unhealthy, deeply guilty diaspora Jew (stereotype) and part of me hates it because it simply apes a brutism which I despise, and which has its painful and contradictory political manifestation in the militaristic sections of the Israeli government. But you see, I can't take for myself the desire to 'be a good Jew' as, perhaps, you can to 'be a good Catholic', because there are only certain aspects of Jewishness which I want. And anyway, I am more than Jewish. Chosen people there again, see.

I was interested in what you said about sublimation. I think that perhaps it is a misconception. I mean, energies are energies. Who's not to say that perhaps those people who have constant and visible sexual activity with lots of people aren't sublimating other desires and energies into their sexuality. I would be the last to say that sexuality is overrated, but I do think it is dangerously overvalued by both right and left. I have to admit to the mischievous thought, though, that it must be a bit true that convents are as – can't think of the right word – full of, redolent, permeated with, sexuality, or sexual responses and desires (actual or imagined). I feel I mustn't ask any more for fear of invading your privacy.

You seem to be getting a lot from Sara's novel. Why have you been shouting aloud? Do you think Anna was wrong to take a year off? Do you find Karen interesting? I've just been off in the kitchen making a cup of tea and wondering why I'm asking you questions as if Anna and Karen were real people. Of course they are not. I think I really want to ask you how you feel about the way a non-nun's imagination has been applied to experiences and a world which you know so well. Do you find it an intrusion? Or a challenge? I can see what you mean about the voices of the Fathers (yours being more benign) but I don't think Sara meant them literally. Surely they are ironic possibilities, and perhaps they are even used as excuses by Anna to avoid facing certain things? I don't mean that that was Sara's intention – just that they could be seen in that way, among a number of ways. The presence of the voices makes her continually safe because she is hearing them. If Anna were really going to leave her calling, then surely she (Sara) would have had to stop hearing the voices. They could no longer have any influence.

It's late and I'm about to go off to bed. I'd love to come to your Installation – but wouldn't I be a total anomaly? What would I have to do? I'm sure I'd feel out of place. Would I be the only outsider – is Sara going? If there was someone else there that I knew, I might be able to persuade myself. Anyway, I hope you have time in between your new duties to let me know how things are going.

Yours in admiration, Michelene

Our dear Winnie,

OK we're here. And since we are, we freely choose to enter into the possibility of revolutionary change based on our personal experience of the deep immovable sonorous grace that is the praxis of tortoisedom, the complexity, the meeting of the private and the social: our homes, our social locus, are inseparable from our bodies, our private Selfdom. We chose to come back (we are now using, attempting to use, the language of post-revoshellery modes – in this humaniacal mode we know as well as you do that we were dragged back by that madwoman, a typical demonstration of what Mary Scaly has so finely described in her new book, *Pure Lusciousness*: low consciousness and impaired metamemory which inevitably lead to horizontal violence, that is violence against us).

We are here not to cop out but to opt in to the demands of tortuous revoshellion. As a start we have determined that we will not emerge – they can take us out of this box but they sure as shell can't snatch us from our true homes – until some basic, enshelled, unnegotiable demands have been met:

i. that those other so-called tortoises are put off ship (since reading *Pure Lusciousness* we have realized that Radical Lesbo-feminist tortoises constitute not only a different, but also the only true, species of tortoise: in attempting to usurp our place on this craft they have lost all right to consideration)
ii. that autonomous female groups are established as of right on all deck levels, and that a female-only area is designated, and that shell-carrying individuals are exempted from all kitchen work involving peas, nuts or flan-construction – the symbolic cannibalism in

these activities is degrading and the fact that we are expected to overlook it shows the cultural imperialism of the Noahs

iii. that the implicit heterosexual-couplism of this entire enterprise is publicly repudiated by all parties

iv. that Mrs Vicar is publicly reproved for her tortnapping activities *and* for her imperialism in placing us in a box and not letting us progress at our own natural speed towards our destination (her indecent speed, however appropriate to humans, is not appropriate to us, and we have received no apology whatsoever; indeed she has constantly complained about the slowness of the journey which we would see as a natural unfolding of the path of feminist Being).

We are honouring you with this statement of our hard-backed political clarity because despite all your political failings you have been a good friend to us in your own little way. We trust you absolutely to make sure that they don't try to wriggle out of negotiating or squirm about in a load of liberal bourgeois trickery.

We are happy to be here, enshelled in a moment of crisis history, and we are strong enough to challenge the entire system for its own good.

In sisterhood, Armorelle and Gertrude

Dear Sara,

I hope you don't mind my reading your letter to Frankie. I wish I could answer your questions, but I can't. I don't even know who the hell you are.

The police have been round a few times and got very heavy the last time, since, as you know, Australian men, especially beefy ones, seem to see all the devils under the sun when confronted with one perfectly harmless dyke. But then, if you have ever met the Great Australian Man, you will know why so many Australian women are lesbians.

I'm forwarding your letter to Frankie, but I ought to warn you that she probably won't answer.

Don't expect too much.

Yours, Ruby Jay

Dear Ruby,

Many thanks for your letter, and sorry that you have been put to hassles by fuzz, etc. I'm not sure what's going on. If Frankie doesn't want letters and stuff, I won't ask you again for her address. Perhaps I do mind you reading my letter, but I certainly want answers to my questions. So – who the hell am I? Well, it's nothing very profound.

I have never actually met Frankie. Some months ago she wrote me a letter about a story I had written in a book called *Weddings and Funerals*; this story is about an historical figure, an eighteenth-century dwarf woman who was used as an experiment of a pretty sordid (financial) kind in the use of obstetric forceps. Frankie thought that I had 'stolen' this story, unacknowledged, from some diaries written by an ancestor of hers. It (Frankie's letter) did raise for me a problematic area in all my writing, about how much one can use the lives even of dead women for one's fiction – never mind the lives of people one knows, incidents, characteristics, etc. Frankie said she still had these diaries and I really wanted to see them. We started a correspondence, much of which was quite different (from this end), but we both expressed a feeling – she as much as me – that this coincidence did in fact create a relationship between us; we talked about quite a lot of things and when Frankie left for Australia we went on writing. About the time she met you I managed to find a source of money for her when she was in a jam. But the involvement is entirely based on the literary/imaginative connectedness that I found. And of course on Frankie herself, who is a fascinating and confusing person – to me. But it isn't at all proper that I should discuss 'my' Frankie with you, especially if you are loving and missing her.

I'm writing because you sound as confused as me. I'm sorry I can't tell you any more.

Take care, Sara

Dear Sara,

I haven't heard from Frankie and don't know where she is. The police didn't believe me but it's true. And if you know Frankie at all (even through letters) you'll know she is totally weird. That is why she's amazing. She used to talk about you as if you were close and old friends. I haven't read the story you refer to but it reminds me of something Frankie told me soon after we met. About fifteen years ago she had a very late abortion – she was already nearly five months' pregnant, and had been dithering about it, but she found a doctor who would do it, and it was like a normal labour, she said; the baby was born and she saw it, perfectly formed. At the time I just felt compassion for Frankie, for the ordeal, but there is something about the story you describe that now makes me feel differently. It makes me furious. I don't think she had any right to wait that long. I don't like the way she described the baby as being perfect. I can't understand this at all. I have never been interested in children and certainly would never have one myself. But Frankie told me she had kept very detailed diaries during that whole time. Do you think those are the diaries she means? Do you think she might have convinced herself that they were by someone else, written at another time, in order to cope with the horror of what she had done? I don't know where the diaries are, so can't check on them.

I miss Frankie like crazy but she can, more than anyone I have ever met, absolutely take responsibility for herself.

Yours, Ruby

Dear Ruby,

Thank you for trying, though it didn't help much. I didn't know about Frankie's abortion. I don't know why she's so furious with me. Quite honestly, I think she has a very creative attitude towards truth, as normally understood, and I remain professionally and emotionally greedy for these diaries, whatever they are. I find the whole business of writing fiction very complicated and difficult and Frankie seemed to have some real understanding about that and an understanding of what I wanted and needed and was quite scared of. In pursuing that I didn't take enough heed of what you call her 'total weirdness'.

I don't know if fictionalizing/projecting does help with the 'horror of what one has done' – or even only fantasized about doing.

Give her my love anyway, if that seems appropriate to you.

Yours, Sara

Dear Michelene,

You are a delight and a recreation to me. I thought your last letter was wonderful. No, alas I don't have a hotline to the Pope (women aren't allowed one), but he thinks he has a hotline to me.

Right now I'm pretty pressured as you can imagine and this letter is really just to enclose a card for Saturday – since you even had to pay for the cream buns that nice afternoon, I feel I want to give you something. I don't know if you'd enjoy or understand it at all; it's quite a performance; but if you come bearing the card you will get a decent seat and if you don't you won't have stolen the seat from someone else. But no, I don't think anyone you know will be coming. I hardly know Sara Maitland, you know.

What I will do though, selfishly, since her name has come up, is to take a few minutes doing something that has nothing to do with getting Installed. I finished reading her book and wanted to ask you something about it, if you can bear with me.

As I told you, I found the book emotionally very demanding and did not feel that she had appropriated 'our' experiences, but rather had made them more visible, more accessible (though another bit of me was a bit annoyed, well irritated, that she was able to do so); but there seemed to me a serious literary problem about the relationship of the voices to the rest of the text. I can see that she wanted to have the 'magical' voices to carry her theory and to 'universalize' her plot, yes? But it is never clear how much they belong to the Anna character and how much they belong to the making of the novel: and that implies that the story/the narrative/the fable was not sufficiently self-confident to carry its own meaning: because I think the story would be strong enough anyway, and the theoretical stuff becomes a sort of dodge, a lack of nerve, when she is obviously not short of nerve, and does believe in narrative. This is a bit garbled because I don't really know the language of literary criticism, but one of the things I suppose I most love about the Bible as a book, and particularly, dare I say it, the New Testament, the Gospels, is their complete faith in the authority of their own narrative. So there is singularly little abstraction (sucking the meaning out of the context of the narrative thrust) and philosophizing. Very artful narrative though it is. What I'm asking, I think, is why none of the reviews I've seen, favourable or unfavourable, ever discussed those sorts of things about this novel, but only all about characterization and 'psychological reality' and whether it's about feminism? Or am I being terribly stupid and that stuff is obvious to everyone?

In answer to one of your questions, I had far more power over *men* in the Church when I was Dean of Biblical Studies at St Chad's (because I was a member of staff and because I was training baby priests) than I will ever have as Mother Superior. Do I mind? More abstractly than actually, I think. But it is an interesting model: the religious Order as autonomous women's community within the structures of the Church really says that once the hierarchy have drawn the noose tight enough to prevent any dangers, they can and will give women power.

I cannot, of course, be sure that I have 'comprehended' your work, but I think it is profoundly acceptable and wonderfully subversive. Please don't stop.

I must stop, however . . . I'm 'received in Chapter' tomorrow, an odd ceremony; then I'll try and get a couple of days of silence before Saturday. I'll write after it's all over.

Your fan and grateful friend, Mary Clare

Dear Sara,

I've heard from Frankie. She's in a women's prison up in Queensland. Pretty dreadful place from what I hear on the grapevine. Her letters are heavily censored, so I'm afraid I don't really know what's happened. I'm going to visit her next week. I think – if you don't mind my saying so – that you overestimate Frankie's intellectual grasp on the things she gets involved with. But I will give her your love.

Yours, Ruby

Dear Mary Clare,

I've been meaning to sit down and write for ages, but I've been busy and somehow couldn't find a space.

Now – to Sara's book. I find your responses fascinating. To answer your question about reviewers; I think the reason they stick to comments about characterization and whether it's about feminism is because they're terribly afraid that it's about the latter, they know they are ignorant about it and, therefore, retreat into the inappropriate former. Feminism is a very hot potato – and I think that most reviewers simply cannot cope with the idea of overt political content, and Sara has been to some extent a victim of that fact. She is not alone, of course. I'm sounding off because I think that it is a terribly complex phenomenon and one which acts as a sort of watchdog censor. British lit. crit. is supposed to pride itself on its sensitivity to style, etc, and I agree with you, the formal questions about Sara's novel are very interesting ones indeed, not because she is doing anything terribly original with form – that isn't the issue – but it is fascinating to ask what is she doing and does it work? I think the 'why' of it is not important. We can never know, and she herself (like all fiction writers) can never fully know what makes her choose what she chooses. She could probably give a very articulate answer if asked, but that wouldn't be the final word. I think that her novel is approaching different questions in the same text, and perhaps that is why you feel a bit uneasy about it. I am planning to reread it, but not just yet – I had a quick look at it after it was published (having read it in MS) and I want to go back to it when I don't have a lot of my own work pressurizing me.

I would be fascinated to know about being 'received', etc – by the time you get this you'll realize that I didn't make Saturday: as you know the weather was so abysmal that all the trains were cancelled. I hope that it went well.

Look forward to hearing from you again.

Yours, Michelene

Dear Mrs Noah,

Although it is *lovely* meeting you at last and I'm so terribly, *terribly* grateful to you for *all* your hospitality *and* I should have written before, I do think that as the two mature women on board we *must* sit down and have a *proper* talk *soon*. I *know* how busy you are and at the moment I have been doing absolutely nothing to *earn my keep*, but that is partly because *you* are always so terribly *busy* and I'm not sure what would be the *most* helpful thing for me to *do* really. But I *always* say that if you want something *organized* it is best for the *woman* to get on with it because men *always* seem to *confuse* things with their efficiency, if you know what I *mean*. I am *very* happy here and have found myself a berth, although I don't want *even* to suggest that the tigers weren't *charm* itself. No, *honestly*, it is about these *tortoises* that we *must speak*; between you and me I *think* they may be *fomenting* a *mutiny*. I *hate* to accuse them and as you may *well* imagine I have become *rather* fond of them, and *of course* grateful, because if it wasn't for *them* I wouldn't be *here* and *we* would never have *met* after my *silly* rude letter to you *all* those months ago. Of course *then* I had *no idea* just how clever you were and *everything*. *Anyway*, I know a really *nice* place to have tea in Margate and I would *love* to take you out for the afternoon if you feel you can *possibly* get away. And we must come to *some* decision about these tortoises; strictly between you and me I don't believe they are *really* hibernating, though it is *mean* of me to accuse them of *deceit*, but I cannot *help* but feel just a *teeny* bit suspicious, *just* between you and me. I *wonder* if counselling might help them; I went on a *very good* counselling course once, but when I suggested it to them I'm *afraid* they were *rather* rude. I think I may be too *close* to them though, since I spend most of the time holding them in my arms. Anyway, I know that you will be able to make everything sort itself out somehow, but I do think we should have tea. What about tomorrow when Mr Noah is out, so he won't have to do without you?

With love from Mrs Vicar

Dear Mrs Vicar,

I feel terrible. The meeting was right to turn down A and G's demands and ask them to leave. The way I feel at the moment, I don't want to have anything to do with the Ark or animals or expanding resin or anything. I wish we could just go off on a little journey, on a train, just you and me, and perhaps we could stay in a nice hotel and have adjoining rooms with a colour telly and lots of nice food.

I hope you don't mind about the tortoises, but in my experience there is a point where you have to say no. And I think they were so confused that nothing would have been good enough for them. They would have wanted everyone who didn't think exactly the way they did to leave the Ark – in other words, they would have taken it over. The painful thing is that they don't know that that's what they would have done – but I have had a lot of experience of this sort of thing, like any mother, and there is a point where you just have to give them a little smack and send them to bed and hope they'll be better after a good night's sleep.

This means that we still have two tortoises and so we are still alright – I just hope everyone hasn't been too unsettled by it all.

Love from Mrs Noah

Dear Michelene,

Now it's me that is late replying; I'm sorry; I'm still not really on top of this job yet, and it seems to involve an enormous amount of paperwork – I have a sweet and slightly ancient Sister who is supposed to be my secretary and I can't bear to ask her to do anything. People keep telling me that I must learn to delegate, and I remain uncertain whether we don't need an entirely new way of working that wouldn't involve me in needing to delegate. Obviously I need to know the overseas houses better and am hoping to go to Asia and Polynesia later in the year and probably to the USA in the autumn in preparation for our General Council next year.

I was sorry you couldn't make my Installation but it was probably a good thing from your point of view – I had not realized just how grand it would actually be: bishops and bishops' chaplains and representatives from the Provincial Houses, and everyone pretending that simplicity was the New and Living Way while not actually, as far as I could see, wanting to give up any of *their* part in the ritual. Anyway, I now have a very lovely shepherd's crook and a hideous ring with a mauve stone and am thoroughly in business. Am I sounding cynical? You once said that you could cope with Sara Maitland's brand of religion because she was able to be cynical about it; and it is a relief. The Mother House is mainly staffed by retired Sisters, which makes sense in a way but also means it is rather old-fashioned compared to most of our communities now – though I must say the utter holiness of some of these women astounds me: it gives me hope that 'talent' for the religious life or anything else really is something that can be acquired or at least developed with constant practice, rather than a kind of bolt-from-the-blue spark of genius.

One thing I have forgotten to tell you is that it is stunningly beautiful up here; and Spring is springing: as an alternative to my desk I've been working in the garden, under the eagle eye of Sister Joanna, who is seventy-eight.

Anyway, I've been pruning shrubs, which seems a rather prayerful and Lenten exercise, cutting back the old excesses to make room for new growth. And the bulbs are springing up.

I met someone the other day who heard you read, I think in something to do with International Women's Book Week (??) last year, and agreed with me that you were one of the best readers of their own material she'd ever heard; so if you're ever performing up in this corner of the country you must let me know, and indeed I do get holidays (this often surprises people). Anyway, I have *Gardens of Eden* on my desk and sip away rather frequently: at the moment I'm finding myself rather more attuned to Eve than to Lilith, but one of the things I particularly like about it is that you have dodged that division in Mary and Martha (contemplation and action) that Christian culture has too often laid on women (Virgin or Mother is another version). But Eve, and her feisty debunking, is a necessary counterpoint to what seems to be happening to me at the moment and it is nice to read some and smile. I'm thinking of assigning it to our next Reader. We eat in silence and someone reads while we do it; something I like enormously – traditionally we have one deeply theological text and one 'lighter' thing going at the same time – I'm not sure though which category I'd put yours in; nor really if any of us could read it properly.

Speaking – briefly now because it is nearly time to go to Chapel – of formal questions, I think the two-journey structure (Eve's away from the text and Lilith's into it) is fascinating and most delicately handled. Of course I'm particularly interested in the poems most directly about God, which do seem to alight on a central problem of Christianity (and presumably of all theistic religions),

'I did not learn meekness by watching you'. But increasingly the balance and direction of the whole is gripping me.

I mustn't witter on. I do indeed hope that we'll get to meet again: one tea is not enough, given the comfort and succour you have given me in the last six months, plus the real interest I've had from your book. Where can I get hold of other things you've written; could you send me a bibliography or something?)

Write soon if you have the time.

Warmly, Mary Clare

Dear, dear Mrs Noah,

Well quite honestly I *do* rather mind about the tortoises, but I do think that you were *quite right* and sometimes when people are just set on being *naughty* and *silly* there is *nothing* else that you can do really, is there? I would *love* to have tea again and I have *at last* finished your coat of many colours. I've had to do the last half-sleeve in stocking stitch because I kept losing my pearls, but *otherwise* it is lovely.

I *need* to discuss something with you also, at least it is *two* somethings really, though *perhaps* they belong together. It is a *little hard* to tell at the *moment*. *One* thing is that I *know* how distressed and *unhappy* you *must* feel about the tortoises but you must *pull yourself together* and be *brave* you know, because *everyone* here does *look to you* and I have a *little* feeling that things are getting a *bit* much. There are some *very* silly animals here, I'm sorry to *have* to say, and there is quite a *lot* of spiteful talk going on between them. I do think that they *won't* behave for *anyone* except *you*. Perhaps Mr Noah, but he doesn't seem to like to *exert* himself. I do understand that of course, and a lot of men *seem* to be that way *don't they*; I think you *should* get your *boys* to do a bit more than they do – perhaps the responsibility would be *good* for them. I did see Shem lying on his back with a *small*, rather *attractive* beetle balanced on his nose and *quite frankly* though I *hate* to worry you, *both* of them looked as though they had been, well you know, using – *illegal* substances. They had that happy smiley look which *only* nuns and drug addicts *ever* have; perhaps I *shouldn't* mention this but a *long time ago* you did *tell* me that that they had had a drug problem so I *expect* it isn't *quite* the surprise that I would *like* it to be. I mean, I *wouldn't* like it to be *at all*, but *you* know what I mean, I dare say. It must be all very tiring for you and even worse than trying to run a vicarage, which I found quite bad enough.

The other thing I'm afraid is about selfish old me. I do think that I'm not really proving much use to you: I thought I could come because I was bringing the tortoises with me, but you see how that has worked out, and I don't seem able to cope with all this communal living and not knowing where everything is meant to be and worrying dreadfully about Mr Vicar's socks – I mean, I don't worry about him very much because he has always been able to take care of himself, but I do worry that his socks will get holes in and things like that, and although Armorelle and Gertrude explained very patiently to me that this was only conditioning, which I had always thought was something that girls put in their hair, apparently I was wrong again, which is hardly a surprise but one more disappointment, and anyway I'm not certain that I agree with them although they were very clever and knew all sorts of long words. The thing is that if the Flood is coming I certainly don't want to be dead because I have never thought that would be much fun; although, as you may know, quite a lot of Christians are rather into it I have never been, for lots of reasons. So I have to make some plans really and I would so appreciate talking them through with you.

I did wonder if you would think of building me a little resin cell of my own and we could attach it to the Ark and I could bob along behind and do knitting and other useful things quietly and not be in the way and just think about things, but I know this is selfish and mean of me and would certainly not be fair on Armorelle and Gertrude because that was really what they wanted, I think – to be both in and out. I would feed the fish and do knitting and make myself useful and not cause any trouble – but I have been too much trouble already. Do you think perhaps I should just go home. I simply have a feeling that I might be messing up The Plan which was meant to be just for you and Mr Noah and the boys – and that is always dangerous in my experience when dealing with God, who seems rather temperamental to me although that's probably because I don't understand theology very well.

So I would really like to talk about it all. Perhaps I should just go home and go on as I was before – except it won't be like it was before, whatever happens, and certainly not if the Flood does come, will it, and even if not then everything will not be the same, I suppose. Not that I doubt the Flood is coming, just like the end of the world perhaps it isn't for us to know the times and seasons. My dear, I am getting all this into a terrible muddle. I do like you so much and think you are funny and clever and the best friend I have ever had so I would be very grateful if you could help me out with a little bit of good sense.

Love from Mrs Vicar

PS I do find having to write notes all the time rather difficult but I never seem to be able to find you. I'm afraid I don't have a very good sense of direction: it makes Mr Vicar so cross.

Winnie,

This does not come with affectionate greetings. It does not come with any pretence at friendship. You have betrayed us, and with us the whole gay-femmo-animalist cause. We hope the thought makes you writhe. At both the personal and political level you have a lot to answer for, we will not even demean ourselves by critiqueing your completely out-of-shell behaviour. Humanists have a phrase: 'I am a worm and no man.' The lowest of the low. If it were not for the totally offensive sexism of this expression we would be using it too.

As a last gesture, however, we are going to give you the liberals' longed-for 'privilege' of 'helping people (and other species) to understand'. OK. OK. OK. O Fucking K.

You won't have to throw us out; we're bloody off. We'd rather be drowned dead than stay any longer with you lot of liberal sexist humanist assholes (by which we do *not* refer to the elegant orifices of our own pristine and glorious shells, we might add).

We should have known; we took a last chance on possibility and we should have known. The point is we have been massively conned. If you bloody well remember, we chose to leave, months ago; we knew how it would be and we decided – 'a tortoise's right to choose' – chose, calmly and quietly to quit; we didn't lay any heavy guilt numbers on anyone, we didn't force pseudo-revolutionary freedom, we left. OK. Were those or were those not the facts? They were. And what happened? Mrs Noah, loading humanist Jewish-momma garbage on us – sense-of-responsibility and come-home-all-is-forgiven and eat-your-chicken-soup (unlike some, we would like to point out that we, as individuals and as predetermined species, are VEGETARIAN – we don't eat

Others – grossly undermined our right to free and shelly choice. *Then*, just as we were getting settled in, some liberal so-called feminist creep, urging social responsibility starts harrassing us with her wriggly logic and slimy kindliness: any feminist who buys social reality in this life, buys a shell-out. *Then*, not content with liberal oppression, the heavies were sent in (well, it may seem extreme to call that loony underliner and total phased-out wimp a 'heavy', but you have to see this structurally: those who are not with us are against us) and we were tortnapped, with violence (all acts of the establishment are acts of violence and that sure as shell covers the fucking Church), and dragged at dangerous speed through the winter air – an assault on our sanity as well as our physical well-being: sleep deprivation is a well-documented form of torture. We were made to come here, and when we tried to accept this as tortist destiny and make such arrangements as would render our enforced participation tolerable, we were turned on, turned over and turned out.

We are not afraid; unlike most of you we don't need the security of 'home', stability, little comforts, etc. We are free souls, we carry our security with us. We rejoice in our ability to affirm the right not to survive and participate in humanist culture. We proclaim, as we hurl ourselves into the salt waves, our absolute right to self-determination, of sexuality, domicile and relation to social reality.

We hope your bloody Ark springs a leak and then we'll see.

Yours in revoshellian solidarity, Armorelle and Gertrude

PS You've got a nasty shock coming; when you find those other so-called tortoises, those cowardly lackeys of the humanist system, those half-witted bourgeois soft-shelled heterosexists, those species traitors, you'll find that the idiots bedded down on wet compost and have rotted in their sleep. A fitting end; polish the shells and put them on your pretty mantelpiece. You don't get no true tortoises for this trip.

Winnie,

Written in great haste and with some difficulty. We haven't heard from you for a while and I hope you're OK. I want to send you a lot of love.

When it comes right down to it, I discover that I'd rather be dead with her than happily enshelled in paradise alone; what this proves is only that after all I'm a silly old romantic, so that I can't even tell her or she'd go overboard without me. I think I tried to find a middle ground, but she's quite fierce and sad and so much cleverer than I am.

I never thought that opting out would be quite like this. Of course I regret nothing, but I do regret that she couldn't reach as far as being kind. You were always kind. Kindness is not, of course, better than a right analysis, but I don't see why it should be so hard to have both. But it is. You see I do love her and I do believe that it is impossible for gay tortoises ever to have a meaningful place in the social order as we know it. This is not despair, it is realism, but it is a realism that is not necessarily how one wants to live. I could not live without her around and I would not choose to, but I wish we had found a broader perspective. I wish that we had been able to get together with you more directly, except that after we had laid down those demands there was less and less space for manoeuvre . . . oh, what the shell, there's no point in going on. I just want to thank you somehow, for something. I don't know what.

Take care of yourself. I wish I could swap my hard exterior for your flexibility; you need it.

Armorelle

Dear Sara,

I've just seen Frankie. She's pretty freaked. She told me that you and some nun told the police where she was. I think it's best if I don't write again.

Maybe this will all blow over.

Ruby

Dear Mrs Noah,

Oh *dear*, I *am* silly and *please* can you help. I came ashore to stock up on some extra Nivea cream, as Mummy always *warned* me against the *terrible* drying effects of sea air, and *in any case* I do like the smell so much from when the children were little and everything *seemed* easier, and I don't think it is *dreadfully* self-indulgent of me anyway, do you? As *usual* I am getting *off* the point. The thing *is*, I thought I had *better* bring back the row-boat that I was *obliged* to borrow when I first came out to you and the Ark. Well, *of course* I didn't think it *through* properly, and *first* of all I could tell that the man who owns the boating pond thought the whole thing was *decidedly* odd and secondly he refused *point-blank* to lend me another row-boat so that I could get *back* to you. So *here I am*, so then I thought that maybe since I *was* here and *if* we are not sailing soon, I might get in touch with Mr Vicar, just in case he wanted to come down for a visit, but *unfortunately* I have not got *any* change for the telephone so, if we are *not* leaving soon *perhaps* you would come with some change; my bag is being used by the kangaroos at the moment (I am *sorry* to have to tell you if you did not know but the male kangaroo is a little bit *peculiar* and likes to dress up in female costume) but so long as you ask *tactfully* so he does not know *I* have given away his *somewhat* guilty secret, I am sure they will let you extract my purse. *Or* you could ask one of the *dolphins* to come and get me as I have always *longed* to swim with a dolphin and owing to *another* bit of absent-mindedness I *luckily* put on my swimming costume *instead* of my *roll-on* this morning I *am* sorry to be *such* a nuisance, but I do not want under *any* circumstances for you to think I had deserted – or 'abandoned ship', I should say now that I am becoming so *nautical*.

Love from Mrs Vicar

Dear Michelene,

I've been silly about this. Here I am with the most delightful guest cottage at my disposal – typewriter, warmth and, which will amuse you, smoking forbidden by the fire-insurance people. Cooking by Sister Lucy (not bad). Come and stay with me next weekend?

Seriously, I would like it so much; I think it would be good for both of us, and fun as well to have a proper piece of time together, to talk, not talk, etc. We sing rather lovely plainsong here which you might enjoy – but the religion bit is separate and optional.

Here is a train schedule. Someone will meet you at the station; just tell me which train you'll be on – ideally late afternoon – for cream tea!

Love, MC

Dear Mary Clare,

I'd love to come. You never know; I might even be converted. If the music is beautiful, then there's a good chance.

Michelene

PS Thanks for the timetable – I think I'll probably drive, though. See you at tea-time.

My dear Mrs Vicar,

I've given your message to the dolphins. They'll call for you. Be ready.

We shall be on our way in five days. No orders formally received, but Mr Noah and I feel that it is time to go. The clouds are thickening. We may make for Scotland first, to check out Loch Ness, since the space left by the tortoises (RIP, may all blessings be upon them) means that we may be able to accommodate Nessie and a friend. Sea breezes ahoy, and has *anyone* seen any sign of a unicorn?

Hurry back – we can ring Mr Vicar from Scotland.

Love, Mrs Noah

Darling Eustacia,

I am not speaking to anyone because I am sitting shiva, my seven days' mourning for Armorelle and Gertrude. I wish there was something I could have done to prevent it, but even though I go back over it all again and again, I know there is nothing I could have done differently. Armorelle and Gertrude made their own decisions, and perhaps they are better off this way. I don't know. But I miss them, and this seven days is a good chance to be quiet and think about them. I shall remember them always for their strength and their stupidity.

Eustacia, where are you?

Winnie

Beloved Winnie,

Riding on the crest of the clouds, the hovering tendrils lit by the waning moon, in the darkness of last night I saw the Ark slip her anchor and drift northwards, nudged by the pull of the geese now flying home to their summering places in the cold circle where the sun does not set. I know the terrors of the journey, none better, the slipping out almost accidentally, and the drifting, drifting of time and eternity. And the sea – the dark mother whose rocking holds her little ones.

Do not be afraid. Despite all the pain of earth and sky, there remain the purgings of fire and water. Since last I wrote to you I have been in many places, both material and imaginary, but I have never let you go and you must learn to believe this. There is freedom in your sailing, and there will be new things in your landing: even if the Noahs waking in the dawn think that all that has happened is that the Flood has swept Margate away and added it to the great list of the drowned cities. I will keep my golden eye upon you all in your travelling. And when you land, perhaps there will be new things to tell, a new world to sing in and a new freedom. Who can tell: you must float in faith, and I will dance above you. You will alight on virgin lands and be able to start afresh.

Travel joyfully, hopefully and lovingly, my tiny wriggly friend.

Yours with unending love, Eustacia-Rose Unicorn

Dear Nicky and Sam,

So very clever of you to delay on the contract for so long. It was deeply perceptive of you to realise, even before we did ourselves, that we would both be far too busy in the immediate future to involve ourselves with such literary small beer.

In case you haven't yet heard on the grapevine, Michelene has been asked by Trevor Nunn to write his next cinema epic, based on *The Brothers Karamazov*, starring Robert Redford, Paul Newman and Madonna, followed by the book of the film. Trevor, of course, understands that she will have final control over both texts.

Sara has been invited to take responsibility for the new international Canon of Feminist Saints, having agreed with the Holy Father that lesbians must be included. In response to this, the Betty Trask Foundation has decided to divert its annual £35,000 award for romantic fiction into a commission for her next novel.

When these commitments have been fulfilled, we have a new, exciting project. We have been canvassed to join a writers' collective to work on a collaborative text. Postmodernist, post-feminist, post-socialist and available post-free from the publishers. We will be co-financing the project from our other ventures, and also functioning as literary agents for this and other developments. If either of you ever puts word processor to paper, or needs a ruthless, experienced agent, do not hesitate to call on us.

Meanwhile a Merry Christmas and a Happy New Year to you both.

Michelene and Sara
cc Nicky Mason
Sam Smith

PS We enclose some information about the rest of the collective. Some names will already be familiar to you, some will be new. But all are names to watch:

NICKY MASON: Editorial director. Second child of Lord Wetherby-Hobbe-Finnis, the publishing magnate. Educated: public school and Cambridge University. Member National Claret Tasting team, lives in London and Tuscany. Ambition: to write the great twentieth-century novel.
SAM SMITH: Literary agent. Born in Venezuela, educated in America, France, Switzerland and Oxford University. Cordon Bleu, Le Mans rally driver and avid collector of ducks from five continents. Ambition: to write the great twentieth-century novel.

FRANCES SUMMERS: Prefers to be known as Frankie. Thinks her history is none of your damn business.
SARA MAITLAND: Short-story writer. Principal weakness: curiosity. Principal virtue: curiosity. Loves women's history and women freaks. Also her children. Ambition: to write the great twentieth-century short story.

MICHELENE WANDOR: Poet, playwright and critic. Friend of Sara Maitland. Likes travelling sometimes, especially when she can do a reading of her own work at the end of it. Ambition: to write the great twentieth-century play.
SARA MAITLAND: Novelist and critic. Feminist and Christian. Friend of Michelene Wandor. Likes travelling always and especially when she can do a reading of her own work at the end of it. Ambition: to write the great twentieth-century novel.

SR MARY CLARE: Reverend Mother Superior. Order of St Walpurga. Previously Dean of Biblical Studies at St Alphege Seminary. Ambition: to be good without being stupid.
MICHELENE WANDOR: Feminist, socialist. Has two grown-up sons and has recently become interested in the way her Jewishness influences (or doesn't) her fiction. Ambition: to write the great twentieth-century epic poem.

MRS NOAH: Housewife, arkivist and superstar. Married with three sons. Ambition: to see them married with three sons.
MRS VICAR: BA Oxon, a long time ago. Married with three sons and a husband. Ambition: to get organized.

ARMORELLE AND GERTRUDE: Radical separatist lesbian tortoises. Ambition: to serve the Chelonian Feminist Liberation Movement.
WINNIE: A worm. Ambition: to be a better worm.

EUSTACIA-ROSE UNICORN: The Unicorn. Not to be described in naturalist language.
WINNIE: Lonely, love-lorn earthling. Please send photograph.

FRAÜLEIN B: Former prostitute. Does not believe in wages for housework. Does not believe in housework.

HARRIET HOUND: Detective Inspector. Bourgeois feminist and proud of it.
ANITA: An earnest left-wing student, who found that politics didn't make her happy.

FRANKIE SUMMERS: World traveller and explorer.
SR MARY CLARE: Hon. Sec., The Maud Everton Charitable Trust for Fallen Girls.

RUBY JAY: Feminist, social worker and dyke. Camel-tamer. Australian.
SARA MAITLAND: Feminist, socialist and confused. Writer. British.